"You're giving the puppy to me?" Samantha asked

"It's more like a loan," Ethan hedged. "But you can play with her whenever you want. And you can name her. How 'bout that?"

She managed a smile and a nod. "Okay."

Kat's heart was in her throat. Ethan had known exactly what to do, what to say to calm down Samantha.

"Mommy?" Samantha said. "Can I name the puppy Winnie?"

"Well, let me have a look at her," Kat said, picking up the Dalmatian puppy before taking her spot on the porch swing next to Ethan. "You're going to be a lot of trouble, Winnie."

The puppy tried to lick her nose, and Kat gave her to Sam, who ran across the yard with her. "Samantha obviously has decided that she likes you."

"So bribing her worked?"

"Showing her you really care is what worked."

"I like her, too," Ethan said softly. Then, with a gentle hand on her chin, he tipped Kat's face up toward his, and she knew he was going to kiss her—and she knew she was going to let him.

Dear Reader,

What woman can resist a firefighter? Any guy who voluntarily runs into a burning building is a true hero, and when I set out to write the FIREHOUSE 59 trilogy, I had no lack of inspiration—there's a fire station right around the corner from my house. The guys there were more than happy to enlighten me about their lives.

One trait firefighters have in common is that they like rescuing people. Ethan, the hero in *The Family Rescue*, has this characteristic in spades. But what if the woman he falls in love with doesn't want to be rescued? Kat is so determined to be strong and independent—and I had an awful lot of fun throwing these two together and watching the sparks fly!

I hope you enjoy the story, and I hope you'll stick around to see how Ethan's fellow firefighters, Tony and Priscilla, meet their romantic matches, too.

All best,

Kara Lennox

The Family Rescue
KARA LENNOX

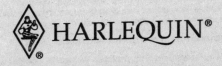

HARLEQUIN®

TORONTO • NEW YORK • LONDON
AMSTERDAM • PARIS • SYDNEY • HAMBURG
STOCKHOLM • ATHENS • TOKYO • MILAN • MADRID
PRAGUE • WARSAW • BUDAPEST • AUCKLAND

ISBN-13: 978-0-373-75150-1
ISBN-10:   0-373-75150-8

THE FAMILY RESCUE

Printed in U.S.A.

ABOUT THE AUTHOR

Texas native Kara Lennox has earned her living at various times as an art director, typesetter, textbook editor and reporter. She's worked in a boutique, a health club and an ad agency. She's been an antiques dealer and even a blackjack dealer. But no work has made her happier than writing romance novels. She has written more than fifty books.

When not writing, Kara indulges in an ever-changing array of hobbies. Her latest passions are bird-watching and long-distance bicycling. She loves to hear from readers; you can visit her Web page at www.karalennox.com.

Books by Kara Lennox

HARLEQUIN AMERICAN ROMANCE

This book is dedicated to firefighters everywhere.
They are the real heroes.

In particular, I would like to thank the
Dallas firefighters at Station 14: Captain Gary Hash,
Driver-Engineer Jim Patton, and Second Driver-
Paramedic Byron Temple. Also, the Dallas firefighters
at Station 11—especially Captain Joe McKenna,
who let me ride on the engine to a real fire and
let me get close enough to feel the spray of the hoses.

Chapter One

At 3:00 a.m., most of the guys at Fire Station 59 were either asleep or watching a cheesy action movie. But for a few of them around the scarred Formica table, fortunes were being won and lost.

"Remind me—does a straight beat a flush, or is it the other way around?" The one woman at the poker table looked at her two opponents with "innocent" big blue eyes.

Ethan Basque suppressed a groan. Talk about beginner's luck! He laid his crummy cards face down on the table. "Doesn't matter, Priscilla. You win again."

"Not so fast," Tony objected. "Pris, sweetie, a flush beats a straight. Do you want to make a bet?"

Priscilla checked her cards and worried her lower lip with her teeth. "Okay." And she pushed all her chips to the center of the table, about twenty bucks' worth.

Tony groaned. "Forget it. You win."

Priscilla smiled sweetly and raked the chips to her side of the table. "Maybe next time you'll let me teach you how to play bridge, instead of insisting on poker."

Ethan laughed at Priscilla's sheer audacity. "Soon you'll be wanting us to drink tea and paint our fingernails." But the comment had no bite. Though not all of his co-workers would agree, he actually liked having a female around the fire station. He and Tony had made it known that anyone who messed with Pris was messing with them, which hadn't made them the most popular guys in a place where rookies were already at a disadvantage.

Tony gathered the cards together and shuffled. "My deal. Seven-card stud, this time. I'm getting my money back."

"If your luck changes." Priscilla arranged her chips into neat, even stacks.

And then the jolting electronic buzz of an alarm filled the station and abruptly ended the game. Tony dropped the cards on the table and three chairs scraped back as the firefighters headed, without a word, to the pole hole.

Ethan's gut tightened as it did every time the alarm sounded. So far, as the three newest members of this company, he and his buddies hadn't faced anything more serious than a smoldering Dumpster, a small kitchen fire and a minor car accident. He'd never even had to stretch hose. But he knew the day they'd trained for was coming, and he anticipated it with both excitement and dread.

Most of the older, more experienced firefighters took the stairs, but the three rookies couldn't resist using the slick brass pole. Station 59 was one of only three in Dallas that still had poles. Ethan landed with perfect control at the bottom, followed quickly by the other two. Each headed for a different vehicle.

Ethan was first to the ladder truck. He stepped into his pants, which were waiting for him by his assigned station. Then he grabbed his coat. Loaded down with forty-plus pounds of turnout gear, he vaulted into the backseat. The ambulance's engine fired up first, and Ethan knew Tony—on paramedic duty—was about to roll out. Tony had been a paramedic for a couple of years before he'd applied to Dallas Fire-Rescue. Priscilla was on the engine. She would be their "nozzle man," on the hose with Otis Granger.

The rest of Ethan's unit boarded the truck, but none of the others acknowledged him. He, Tony and Priscilla were the "probies," the rookies, the untried. At this point there was no trust, no camaraderie.

Not yet. Maybe never.

Lieutenant Murph McCrae rode shotgun in the officer's seat. As a rookie, Ethan's job was to stick close to McCrae, watch and learn. Which wouldn't have been so bad, except McCrae clearly didn't want a rookie at his elbow. The rest of his unit consisted of Captain Eric Campeon, the driver, who would be in charge of their rig, and Bing Tate, a thoroughly obnoxious guy who liked to crack filthy jokes in front of Priscilla in a vain effort to embarrass her.

As the engine rolled, they got the word from dispatch. The second alarm had gone out—which meant their wagon was on its way to a fully involved fire. The truck sped through the streets of Dallas's Oak

Cliff section, and Ethan's heart thundered inside his chest. This was it. He was off to meet the beast—fire.

Fifty-nine wasn't the first company to arrive at the two-story apartment building, where smoke was pouring out of a lower window. The captain from Station 21, now Incident Commander, was already organizing resources and developing strategy. News traveled in shouts and nervous whispers: People were trapped inside.

"We're going inside," the IC bellowed. The firefighters' assignments streaked through the chain of command.

Three hose units went in through the building's front door—"stretching heavy." As he waited in the staging area to get his orders, Ethan watched the hose units. He didn't see Priscilla among them, and he tried not to worry about her.

"McCrae," Captain Campeon ordered, "you and the rookie run a ladder up to the second floor, to that window." He pointed to a dark window at the end of the building, two doors down from the burning unit. "Let the nozzle guys go in first, then follow and initiate a preliminary search-and-rescue."

Ethan was going in.

As Ethan and McCrae pulled a wall ladder off the truck, McCrae was quiet, calm, focused on his task. His movements were swift but controlled. Ethan ordered himself to adopt the same attitude. No panic, no rushing. Mistakes were made when you rushed.

The hose went up first. Otis Granger, a large African-American man Priscilla was assigned to stick close to, climbed the ladder first, dragging another smaller ladder with him. Priscilla followed with the hose. Her pristine beige coat stood out from the others', as did Ethan's. He watched her disappear through the window and said a silent prayer she would be okay.

With his air mask in place, Ethan climbed his first ladder into his first real—post-training—burning building. His knees felt shaky, and every survival instinct he was born with screamed, *No. Go back. Run!* But the instant he climbed through the window, all those months of training took control. He slowed his breathing so he wouldn't suck down thirty minutes of air in ten.

All he had to do was follow Murph McCrae. Murph was a cranky old guy, but everyone said he knew his stuff.

Ethan and McCrae did a preliminary search of the first apartment, following the walls counterclockwise as Otis and Priscilla hatcheted their way through the ceiling. Though smoke had already seeped in, Ethan's flashlight penetrated and visibility was still pretty good. They found no one.

The next apartment was a different story. They chopped a hole through a wall—easier than breaching the locked solid-core door—and stepped in. Smoke met them, pouring through the opening in an opaque cloud. In moments, they were walking into black soup.

"Get down," McCrae ordered, but Ethan was already dropping to his hands and knees, trying not to think about whether the apartment below was involved; whether the floor beneath him was burning. He proceeded around the room, again counterclockwise, feeling along the walls, keeping the reflective stripes of McCrae's pants in view at all times.

"I've got a victim," McCrae reported, his voice sounding way too calm in the radio earpiece, and Ethan's heart pounded inside his chest. His first major fire, and someone's life might depend on the actions he took in the next few seconds.

"Two victims," McCrae corrected himself. "Woman and child. And…Christ almighty, a cat." McCrae had made it clear he didn't like cats.

Ethan quickly crawled forward, finding the victims by feel. "I've got the kid," he said. The tiny girl had a wiggling kitten in her arms, and she wasn't about to let go. Ethan grasped her by the elbows and started dragging, backing out the way he'd come. The child squirmed and cried, and Ethan recognized the pronounced wheezing of an asthmatic. She fought him every step of the way, but he couldn't risk swinging her up into his arms. Even a few feet higher, the temperature could be hot enough to singe skin.

"It's okay, I'm here to help you," he said over and over.

From a few feet away, he could hear the woman coughing and then gasping out, "My baby… Save my baby…first."

"I've got her," Ethan yelled, hoping she could hear him through his oxygen mask and over the chaotic noise of rushing water and crackling fire. Hoping there wasn't a second child somewhere.

"McCrae to Incident Command." Ethan heard the call go out through his earpiece. "We've got two victims, taking them out the window. Requesting assistance."

"Ten-four."

Because the girl was so small, Ethan made quick progress with her, half crawling, half duck-walking as he dragged her along the carpet. She stopped struggling and grew frighteningly quiet.

Hold on. Oh, God. Please, little girl, hold on.

Smoke now filled the apartment, though the open window provided some ventilation. Ethan heard shouting and banging above him—Priscilla and Otis battling the blaze, and others on the roof, opening ventilation holes.

When Ethan reached the window with the child, another firefighter was waiting at the top of the ladder. Ethan quickly stood and passed the frail child—who, amazingly, was still clutching the kitten—through the window. Her breathing was labored, but at least she *was* breathing. Almost as soon as she'd disappeared, another helmet ascended and a pair of gloved hands reached out for the second victim.

Ethan joined McCrae, and together they dragged the woman the rest of the way to the window. Ethan swung her up in his arms, only then getting a glimpse of her blackened face and the tumble of thick, dark hair. Her lids fluttered and she stared up at him, her dark eyes filled with primal fear.

"Samantha?" Her voice was weak.

"We got your little girl. Is she the only one?" Don't let there be more.

"Yes. Please save her."

And in those brief seconds, just before he handed her off to another firefighter, Ethan felt a current run between them. Maybe it was just the adrenaline pumping through his body, but it nearly knocked him off his feet.

McCrae punched him in the shoulder and brought him back to his senses. They had more work to do.

They continued their search-and-rescue but found no other victims, alive or dead.

An airhorn penetrated the sound of the fire and rushing water. That was the signal to clear the premises.

"Move!" McCrae boomed. "This building could go any second!"

Ethan retreated the way he'd come in, through the window, with McCrae right behind him. A loud whoosh and a spray of sparks from the roof indicated a collapse at the other end of the structure.

As Ethan hit the ground, he looked back and up, anxious until he saw Priscilla and Otis emerge.

He spotted a few of the building's residents, in night-clothes or with sheets wrapped around them, staring at the remains of their home with dazed looks on their faces. But the dark-haired woman and her daughter were nowhere to be seen.

They'd probably already gone to the hospital— maybe in Tony's wagon.

He couldn't worry about that now. There was lots more work to be done here.

"Basque!" McCrae yelled. "Help me with the ladder."

For a few seconds, Ethan had forgotten his primary directive—to stick to his senior officer like Velcro. Thankfully McCrae was only a few feet away, and Ethan rejoined him. The aftermath of this fire would consume the rest of his shift. But so would thoughts of a pair of dark, frightened eyes.

BACK AT THE STATION, Ethan jumped down from the engine and peeled off his grimy turnout gear. He was pleased to see that his coat and pants now looked as filthy as everyone else's. He would no longer stand out as a rookie.

It was almost 6:00 a.m. Only an hour left in Ethan's shift. As he hosed off his gear and laid it out to dry, McCrae touched him on the shoulder. "Basque."

"Yes, sir?" Ethan wondered what he'd done wrong.

McCrae wouldn't meet his gaze. "You did good out there. You didn't lose your head."

A warmth spread through Ethan's chest. "Thank you, sir." Later, he would share a private, rowdier, celebration with Tony and Pris. But McCrae's brief praise was a victory.

The rookies had been assigned to this station under conditions that were trying at best. A few months earlier, three men from Station 59 had died in a warehouse fire. The tragedy had sent shock waves through all of Dallas Fire-Rescue—through the entire city, in fact.

If Ethan had heard it once, he'd heard it a dozen

times. No one could fill the boots of those three men. Yet that was exactly what the rookies were trying to do. They'd faced undercurrents of resentment, and sometimes outright hostility, since they'd been assigned to the company two weeks ago.

No one wanted them here.

But Ethan would trust Tony and Priscilla with his life any day. He'd trained alongside them. He'd seen how hard they worked every day. He'd watched Pris struggle with the strength training, working hours and hours on her own time climbing ropes, carrying dummies over walls and down ladders. And Tony—well, Ethan and Tony had been watching each other's backs since they were ten, when a gang of older kids had picked a fight with Tony after school. Ethan hadn't thought twice—he'd jumped in swinging. And though he and Tony had both gotten the snot beat out of them, they'd become instant best friends.

The three rookies trusted each other, and they would simply have to earn the trust of the others, an inch at a time. This shift, Ethan had moved forward the first inch. He was willing to bet Priscilla had, too.

After showering and changing into clean clothes, Ethan found his two friends in the kitchen. Tony was putting the coffee on so that A shift would have a fresh pot when they arrived.

"Hey, the conquering hero," Tony said. "Wish I coulda been inside with you guys, instead of on paramedic duty."

"I can't believe you saved two people," Pris said in a whisper. "Holy cow."

The woman and the girl. Memories of them rushed back into Ethan's mind, along with the crazy sensations he'd felt during the rescue—pride in doing his job, along with fear that he'd do something wrong. "McCrae was there, too, don't forget," he said. "Have you heard if they're okay? I looked for them when I came out, but they were gone."

He'd heard nothing about fatalities, however, so he was hopeful they'd both survived.

"I transported them to Methodist," Tony said. "The mom was okay. The little girl was struggling a bit with her asthma, but I think she'll be fine."

Thank God. Ethan wasn't sure how he would have handled it, if his first rescue had ended badly.

"Which reminds me…" Tony said. "I have something to show you."

Tony walked over to a gym bag that was sitting on the floor, picked it up gingerly and set it on the table, unzipping it in front of Ethan. Inside was the most pathetic-looking kitten Ethan had ever seen, its ears singed, its fur so black with soot that its true color was impossible to tell. Resting on a bed of clean socks, it mewed weakly.

"Can you save it, d'you think?" Tony asked.

Ethan quickly closed the bag. "Are you crazy? If McCrae sees this, he'll pitch a fit."

"I couldn't leave it in the street. You, of all people, should appreciate that." He turned to Priscilla. "When Ethan and I were kids, he was always dragging home half-dead animals, begging his mom to help save their lives."

Ethan grinned. True, usually he was the softhearted one who took in strays—animals *and* people. Tony had been a stray, just one of seven skinny kids in a family with too many mouths to feed. After that first fight, Ethan had taken Tony home, where his mom fussed over both of them, treating their injuries. She insisted Tony stay for dinner—Gloria Basque was even more tenderhearted than Ethan.

Tony had made the Basque house his second home, crashing there whenever things got too intense in his less-than-stable home environment. Sometimes, he'd have a couple of little sisters in tow, and somehow Ethan's mom stretched her dinner to feed them. She was still taking care of strays, and so was Ethan. He'd learned from the best.

The alarm sounded again. Not a fire this time, but a medical emergency. Tony looked at his watch as he headed out the door. "Another fifteen minutes, and I'd have been out of here." With his paramedic background, he was much more sanguine about alarms than Ethan and Priscilla were.

Priscilla went to fold up her bedding and stow it in her locker. Ethan hadn't even made up a bed for that night. Because of the strange environment, the lumpy mattress and a case of nerves, he had a hard time sleeping at the fire station. And frequently, when he did sleep, alarms woke him up—sending adrenaline coursing through his body, even when the call wasn't for Station 59. He figured he'd get used to it eventually.

Ethan peeked into the gym bag. Clearly, the kitten

was scared to death. He stroked its head and it immediately responded. "I'll take care of you until we can return you to your mom," he whispered in a voice he never would have used in front of another guy. He smiled, as he realized he now had the perfect excuse to track down the woman and child he'd rescued.

He just wanted to check on the little girl and see whether she'd recovered. That's what he told himself, anyway. But it was the woman who really intrigued him. Her desperation to save her daughter, the plea in her brown eyes, had gotten under his skin.

"I'D LIKE TO KEEP Samantha under observation for a few more hours."

Kathryn Holiday nodded at the resident who was treating her and her seven-year-old daughter for smoke inhalation and she tried to hold it together. Was something wrong with her baby? She *seemed* okay. Samantha had received two breathing treatments with a nebulizer, which had eased her asthma symptoms considerably. She'd also been treated for some cat scratches on her arms, but they weren't serious. It was a testament to Samantha's grit and determination, that she hadn't let go of the panicked kitten when he scratched her.

With a pang of remorse, she wondered where the kitten was now.

The resident, whose nametag identified her as Dr. Shinn, gave Kat a reassuring smile. She'd been good with Samantha. "Your daughter was slightly disoriented when they brought her in. I want to run a couple of tests and make sure she didn't suffer any lasting ill effects."

Kat nodded. "Whatever you think is best." She had health insurance, but it wasn't a great policy. The deductible was sky-high and she'd probably end up owing thousands, but she couldn't worry about that. She and Samantha were alive, they weren't seriously injured; that was what mattered.

A volunteer had scrounged some clothes for Kat—a T-shirt, ill-fitting jeans and a pair of loafers about ready for the trash bin.

Kat had nearly refused. Memories welled up, awful images of the church ladies who used to bring her cast-off clothes and tut-tut at her horrid apartment. But sanity had prevailed. She couldn't remain barefoot and in a smoke-blackened nightgown.

"We can monitor Samantha in the E.R.," Dr. Shinn continued. "No need to formally admit her."

"Can I stay with her?"

"Of course. I'll see if I can find a cot for you."

Kat nodded her thanks. Everyone had been so kind—the doctors and nurses, the gorgeous Latino paramedic who could have charmed the stripes off a zebra… And the firemen who'd saved her and Samantha.

One fireman, in particular, who'd lifted her up as if she weighed nothing.

Her thoughts had turned to her personal hero, over and over, during the night's ordeal. She and Samantha would have succumbed to the smoke in another couple of minutes, if they hadn't been dragged to safety. She remembered how strong his arms had been as he'd swung her up; how deep and reassuring his voice had been as he'd told her Samantha was safe and everything would be okay. His face had been obscured by an oxygen mask, but he had the kindest brown eyes she'd ever seen.

She had no idea what his name was.

True to her word, the resident found a cot and an orderly dragged it into Samantha's treatment room. Exhausted and aching from her deep coughing Kat curled up under a thin blanket, but she didn't sleep. She listened.

Earlier, Samantha had struggled for every breath. Now, however, she sounded normal and she'd fallen asleep.

Samantha had been so terrified when she'd woken Kat in the middle of the night. The smoke alarm was buzzing, and Kat, who slept like a stone, hadn't heard it. By then, the apartment was filled with smoke and the sounds of approaching sirens. Every fire-safety tip Kat had ever heard flashed through her mind, but all she could think about was escape. Get to the door. Get out.

They would have gotten out in plenty of time, too, if Samantha hadn't suddenly remembered Bashira, the stray kitten they'd taken in only a week earlier. Precious minutes had passed as they searched, finally locating the terrified animal under a bed.

By then, the smoke had grown thick and the air hot, and as she'd struggled for breath, Kat had become confused. She encountered walls in unexpected places, then tripped over a chair. She remembered collapsing, hearing Samantha's terrified cries and groping for her daughter. As the flames danced in her peripheral vision, she remembered praying—not for salvation but that their deaths would be quick.

They'd been so amazingly lucky the firefighters had found them in time. She had to focus on that, rather than on the fact that she'd lost all her material possessions. Things could be replaced.

The door opened and Kat sat up suddenly, realizing she'd been dozing and reliving the fire. She expected to see another nurse or doctor, there to check vital signs. Instead, she saw a tall man with sandy blond hair and almost impossibly wide shoulders standing uncertainly in the doorway. He wore a charcoal gray T-shirt and faded Levi's, and at first Kat thought he must have entered by mistake.

Then she saw the eyes and she realized this was one of her rescuers, the one she remembered most clearly. Her heart jumped as she got her first good look at him, freshly showered and out of his fireman gear.

"How's she doing?" the man asked in a low voice, so as not to wake Samantha. She appreciated this courtesy. Samantha had been scared and fretful each time she woke up in this strange place.

"She's going to be okay." Kat rose from the cot and gestured toward the hallway. The man opened the door wider to let her exit, then followed. "The smoke triggered an asthma attack, but she responded well to treatment. They're just keeping her a few more hours as a precaution."

"And you?" His voice was deep and rich.

"I'm fine." She would keep saying that until she could manage it without flinching. Though she was grateful that Samantha's life and hers had been spared, she was anything but fine. Nothing in her life, so far, had prepared her for the disorientation she felt, the sense that she couldn't look forward but could only live minute-to-minute.

She was homeless. She'd lost her purse, her money and checkbook—all her ID. She might still have a car, but she had no idea where the keys were.

The firefighter guided her to a bench across the hall from the treatment room. "I'm Ethan Basque."

She shook his hand, which seemed ridiculous, given that he'd held her in his arms only a few hours earlier. She'd been wearing nothing but a thin nightgown. "Kathryn Holiday. Kat. I don't know how to begin to thank you for saving our lives."

"It was my job." But then he grinned, and her heart did a little lurch. It took a special kind of person to do what this man had done, to risk his own life to save those of strangers.

"It's good of you to check on us. Do you always take a personal interest in people you rescue?"

He shrugged one muscular shoulder. "So far, one hundred percent. You and your daughter are the first people I ever rescued."

"Really?"

"Your apartment building was my first real fire." He couldn't suppress another grin over this admission, which made Kat's heart give a couple of extra beats.

"You did great," she said. "All of you did."

"I'm sorry we couldn't do more to save your building. But we did save your cat."

Her hand flew to her mouth in surprise. "Bashira! Oh, poor thing. I had no idea what happened to him."

"I took him home with me. He's a little worse for wear, but I think he'll be okay. Anyway, he's safe until you get settled some place. Do you have friends or family you can stay with?"

She deflated a bit. "I guess I won't be going back to my apartment."

"Not anytime soon. We know how the fire started, by the way. Your downstairs neighbor left a cigar burning."

"Is he… Did he get out okay?"

Ethan nodded. "Everyone got out. But your apartment is a total loss. I'm sorry."

She sighed and swallowed back tears. "I guess I knew that."

"Do you have somewhere to go?" he asked again.

"Yes. They'll be releasing Samantha soon, and I can stay with a friend until I find my own place." Kat had already called Deb, her office manager, at work. Deb had offered her a sofa for as long as Kat needed it.

"How about something to eat, then?" Ethan asked.

Kat was tempted. She was beyond stressed out, could hardly think what to do next, and here was this gorgeous guy who was willing to risk his life for perfect strangers, then follow up with still more kindness.

But no, that wasn't the way to handle her dilemma. Didn't she constantly counsel her girls on this very subject? *Learn to get yourself out of trouble. Don't expect some guy to rescue you.* She had a little money in the bank, and renters' insurance would cover at least some of her losses. A locksmith could make her new car keys. Visa would send her a new credit card.

"It's very kind of you to offer, but I have things under control."

Rather than acknowledge her strength, he gave her a cajoling smile. "Give a guy a break. Let me buy you breakfast."

She wavered. Her stomach was empty, and she didn't even have change on her for a vending machine. But then she heard Samantha's voice. "Mommy?" Then, louder. "Mommy?"

Kat jumped to her feet and lunged for the treatment room. "I'm right here, sweetheart." She went to Samantha's bed and ruffled her hair. Her daughter had been washed up pretty well, but she still had a bit of soot in one ear.

"I want to go home," Samantha said, fighting tears.

"I know. It's not very much fun here. But the doctors just want to make sure you're okay, and I do, too." She didn't bother to remind Samantha that they didn't have a home to go to.

Samantha's face gradually relaxed as Kat rubbed her chest.

"Is she okay?" Ethan asked from the doorway.

Kat started to answer, but Samantha's eyes widened when she saw him and she gasped in a deep breath. Her sharp scream split the air.

Panic rising in Kat's throat, she whirled around, her hands locked into fists and saw only Ethan. Confused, she turned back to Samantha, who was crying and still clearly terrified.

Kat gathered the child against her. "Sam, shhh, it's okay. What's wrong? Are you hurting?"

Samantha clung to Kat and buried her face in her mother's shirt. "That man. Make him leave!"

Chapter Two

Ethan backed out of the room as quickly as he could. What was going on? Maybe he wasn't a pretty boy like Tony, but he didn't normally scare small children.

A nurse and two doctors rushed past him into the room, and as Ethan listened at the door, Samantha's crying quieted. Muffled voices said something about Samantha associating a firefighter with the trauma of the fire. How had the child even recognized him? She couldn't have gotten a good look at him in all that smoke, and she'd only seen his face for maybe a second as he'd passed her through the window. Perhaps she'd recognized his voice.

He waited a few more minutes, hoping Kat would come out of the room so he could apologize for upsetting her daughter. But she didn't appear and he didn't dare go back in. Exhaustion was catching up with him. He decided the best route for him was a strategic retreat, a soft bed and several hours of sleep.

He'd done what he'd set out to do. He'd made sure the woman and child were okay. He left his number with one of the nurses, so Kathryn could call when she was ready to reclaim her kitten, who was happily installed in his utility room with food, water and litter.

During training, Ethan had been told by a wise, old captain, now retired, that you should never look a fire victim in the eye. Your heart couldn't go out to every single one or you'd tear yourself to pieces, he'd said. It was a lesson every rookie had to learn—toughen up or get very depressed.

But maybe it had to be learned through experience. Ethan hadn't been able to avoid looking down into Kat's beautiful dark eyes, so frightened, so trusting.

Was this how it would be? Would he feel this urge to involve himself in the lives of every person he helped during a fire? Yeah, he had a soft spot for anyone or anything in trouble. Given the mother he'd been born to, how could he not? He was still close to her, and he would not be able to look her in the eye if he walked away from someone in a jam.

He'd always thought wanting to help people was a good thing.

Reaching for the handle of the glass doors at the front of Methodist Medical Center, Ethan did a double take. Tony was strolling through the adjacent door, looking confident, a certain swagger in his step. He carried a small bunch of grocery-store flowers.

Ethan recognized the signs. His best friend was on the prowl. It had been a few weeks since Tony and his most recent girlfriend had called it quits, and he was a man who liked having a woman in his life. He got antsy when he was unattached, casting around for a likely candidate everywhere he went.

Once he found a woman he was interested in, it didn't take much. A little flirtation, some flowers and *wham*. They usually fell as hard and fast as Tony did.

"Tony."

Tony stopped, and did his own double take. "What are you doing here?"

"I wanted to let Kathryn Holiday know I had her kitten. What's your excuse?"

"Hey, when a woman's that good-looking, do you need an excuse?" But then his cocky grin faded. "She's okay, isn't she? And the little girl?"

"I saw them and they're fine. But Tony…" Ethan thought it prudent to warn his friend. "The little girl wasn't too happy to see me. She was apparently traumatized by the fire, and I reminded her of it. And since you were the one sticking needles in her…"

"I'll go easy. I can at least say hi to Kat."

Kat. The way Tony said it made it sound as if they were already close. "You aren't going to hit on her, are you?"

"Any particular reason I shouldn't?"

Ethan shrugged. It was hell having a best friend who looked like a Gap model and who could charm butterflies out of their cocoons.

"If you've got a thing for this girl," Tony said, "she's all yours. You know I never poach."

Did he? Have a "thing"? Ethan wanted to tell Tony

he wasn't interested, that he'd visited Kat and Samantha at the hospital as a professional courtesy. But he'd have been lying.

SEVERAL HOURS LATER, Ethan was in his backyard, painting his garage. He'd promised himself that once his firefighter training was completed and he got assigned to a station, he would get to work on this eyesore. The two-story detached frame structure, with garage below and a small apartment above, had been added some time in the 1940s. But unlike his hundred-year-old house, which he'd meticulously updated when he bought it a couple of years ago, the garage was a wreck. He'd replaced a few rotting boards and fixed a leaky roof, but he hadn't done much in the way of cosmetic work.

His first step was to paint the garage charcoal-gray to match the house, so at least his neighbors would no longer have to look at the peeling walls. But he still had a lot of finishing work to do inside—painting, plumbing updates, a new kitchen. The wiring was old, but he'd examined it closely and deemed it safe, at least.

Ethan intended to get as much done as he could before he started his paramedic training. All Dallas firefighters had to get their paramedic certification. When the summer term started, much of his time off would be consumed by classroom instruction via computer. He didn't relish sitting for hours at a terminal. But it was necessary, and in a few months he would begin clinical work, which would be more interesting.

"Lookin' good."

The voice came from over the fence. Tony, in the yard next door, wrestled with a new hedge trimmer. He attacked an overgrown row of privet with the critical eye of a sculptor.

Priscilla had bought the house next door when it had come on the market recently. She'd wanted to live closer to the station, which was by pure good fortune just a couple of blocks from Ethan's. And since the large house was divided into two apartments, Priscilla had talked Tony into renting the downstairs unit from her.

Tony had never lived in a place that required yard work. But since moving here he'd discovered the joy of power tools—mowers, trimmers, blowers. He couldn't be stopped.

Ethan ambled over to the fence. "So, how was it?"

"You mean, Kat? It was fine. I gave her the flowers, and she thanked me for taking care of her daughter. I said you're welcome. I said hello to the girl, and then I left."

"You saw Samantha?"

"Yeah. Cute kid. She's only a couple of years younger than Jasmine, but I can hardly remember Jas being that little." Jasmine was Tony's almost-nine-year-old daughter. He'd only been sixteen when his girl-friend, Natalie, found out she was pregnant, and Nat's parents had talked them out of getting married. But he'd always been involved in Jas's life, sharing custody equally with Nat.

"Samantha didn't…scream?" Ethan asked.

"Scream? Nah, she was talking a blue streak, though. Smart kid. I like her." Tony buzzed at the hedge some more, trying to get an even top line.

"Hmm." So Samantha hadn't been afraid of the paramedic who'd poked and prodded her. Only the firefighter who'd dragged her to safety. Ethan didn't really want to hear any more, but for some perverse reason he asked, "Did you get her phone number?"

"Samantha's? I think she's a little young for me."

"Don't be a doofus. Kat's."

"You're the doofus. She doesn't have one. All her phones got burned up." He paused, then added, "Man, you already got it bad for her. Understandable—she's hot."

"Is that all you can think to say about her? She's a lot more than just hot." Yeah, Ethan was attracted. What red-blooded male wouldn't be? But it was her softness, her vulnerability, that really drew him in. The thought that she and her little girl might be all alone in the world. The possibility that she might *need* him.

Did she really have a friend to stay with? Why was no one at the hospital with her? Did she have any money? Her apartment building hadn't been a haven for crack addicts or prostitutes. Certainly there were many worse places to live in Oak Cliff, which featured everything from million-dollar mansions to falling-down shacks. But it hadn't been anything special, either.

He could walk away from a pretty woman. But a wounded bird—that was a different matter.

Tony chuckled. "Just ask her out. It's not that big a deal."

"I'll see how it goes," Ethan said noncommittally. He had no way of getting in touch with Kat. All he could do was wait until she contacted him about her kitten.

And who knew when that might happen?

DURING THE HOURS after the fire, Kat alternated between supreme confidence that she could handle everything and dismal despair that nothing would ever be the same again.

At least Samantha had a safe haven. She would stay with her dad this weekend. When Kat had called her ex and told him about the fire, he'd dropped everything and promised to come to the hospital as fast as he could.

Chuck Ballard was a good guy, a concerned father who was very involved in Samantha's life. There'd never been any question about custody, though. Chuck, a bit old-fashioned, felt that a little girl belonged with her mother. But he always paid his child support on time, and he never missed a weekend visitation.

Even now that he was remarried and the father of a new baby, he made time for Samantha.

"Do I have to go stay with Daddy?" Samantha asked as they sat in front of the hospital in their borrowed clothes, waiting for Chuck to pick them up.

Kat pulled Samantha into her lap. "I thought you loved staying with your dad. Besides, he's really worried about you. He's promised to take the whole day off work and spoil you silly." Kat had called Samantha's school to let them know she would not be attending today, Friday. By Monday, Kat hoped things would be back to normal—or at least not quite so chaotic.

"I do. But I want you to come, too."

"I wish I could. But I have to find us a new place to live. And I have to file a claim with our insurance, so we can buy new furniture and clothes and stuff."

Samantha nodded, perking up slightly. "Can I get a princess bed like Krista's?" Krista was her best friend at school, and she had a "princess" bed with a ruffled canopy.

"You can get any kind of bed you want."

"Will you call me?"

"I will definitely call you. Okay?" She made another mental note: Replace cell phone. Her mental notebook was getting pretty crowded.

"Okay."

Chuck's familiar Subaru pulled up a few minutes later and Chuck leaped out. He was a nice-looking man, tall with a ready smile and thick, dark hair, receding slightly. The mere sight of him had once made Kat feel so safe. Now, she felt only gratitude that he was such a concerned father to Sam.

He scooped Samantha up in his arms. "Oh, Sammy, when I heard what happened I was so scared. Are you sure you're okay?"

"The doctor *said* I was okay."

Chuck reached for Kat and pulled her into a light embrace. "I was worried about you, too, kiddo."

Kat put on a brave smile. "We're fine. Right, Sam? She was very brave."

"Do you have some place to stay?"

"I'm staying with Deb, my office manager. So if you can drop me at the office—"

"You're working? After you lost everything in a fire?"

"I'm borrowing Deb's car."

"You should get some sleep first. You can crash at my place." He said it as if the decision were made.

Kat took a deep breath. This was the main reason they'd gotten divorced. Chuck meant well—he didn't have a mean bone in his body. But he liked taking care of Kat, which included making all her decisions for her. That had been fine when she'd been a seventeen-year-old orphan, scared out of her wits. But it wasn't so fine now that she was a twenty-six-year-old businesswoman.

"No, Chuck, I really need to go to the office. I'll be fine."

He didn't argue further, but he didn't approve, either. She'd learned not to let that bother her. She did not need others' approval to validate her. That was the core value of StrongGirls, a counseling and life-skills program for at-risk teen girls that was Kat's brainchild, and now her livelihood and her passion. Kat had toyed with the idea of starting her own nonprofit before grad school, and she'd gotten serious about it a couple of years ago. She'd designed the curriculum and applied for grants. Last January, she'd opened her doors. Although it was a small program right now, Kat felt it was meeting the objectives she'd set. She was making a difference in young girls' lives.

When they reached her office, a tiny storefront on busy Jefferson Street, she gave Samantha one final hug. "I'm proud of you, sweetie," she said. "I know how tough this is, but you've been a real trouper."

"Am I a StrongGirl?"

"My number-one StrongGirl."

Chuck tried to give Kat some cash, and when she refused he pressed a wad of bills into her hands anyway. That was Chuck. Generous to the point of being pushy about it. But she knew his heart was in the right place. He'd done so much for her during their marriage. He'd been kind and giving and gentle—the exact opposite of the men she'd known growing up.

"I'll pay you back," she said.

"You don't have to," he said with a rueful grin. "But I know you will."

It wasn't until Saturday that Kat had the chance to retrieve her kitten. She'd spent the previous day running around like crazy—having a locksmith make new keys for her car, contacting her insurance agent, buying some clothes, replacing her cell phone and Sam's asthma meds. Then she'd crashed at Deb's place—a tiny efficiency apartment—and had slept for ten hours straight, despite the fact that her "bed" was a hard sofa.

The next morning, feeling more like herself, she pulled from her pocket the crumpled scrap of paper she'd been carrying around like an amulet. As she dialed Ethan's number, she felt a thrill of anticipation. She'd been savoring the thought of this moment ever since she'd been handed his note at the hospital.

"Kat. Is everything okay?" he asked the moment she identified herself. His voice was filled with concern, which made her stomach swoop, but of course he would worry about her. He'd saved her life and probably felt a responsibility to make sure he hadn't saved it for nothing.

"I'm doing great," she said with a bit more enthusiasm than she felt. "How's Bashira?"

"He's good. I gave him a bath to get the soot off his fur. His ears are kinda raggedy."

The thought of a big, strong firefighter trying to bathe her little kitten touched her heart. She wished she could have seen it. "I bet he loved that. How many stitches did you require?"

He laughed, and she tingled at the sound of it. Deep and rich. "No stitches. Bashira's my bud. He's already taken over my house. You want me to bring him to you? I'm off today. Where are you staying?"

"You don't have to bother," she said. "I'll come get him. Would ten o'clock be a good time?"

"Ten is good." He gave her his address in Winnetka Heights, Oak Cliff's historic district. She loved that area, with its tall trees and hundred-year-old houses. Some were showplaces, fixed up and painted in period colors, with thick carpets of green grass and bright flowers planted in front. Some were grim, sagging affairs, waiting for a loving owner to do the urban restoration and fill them with charm. She wondered which type Ethan lived in.

After hanging up, Kat found Deb staring quizzically at her. Deb was just out of college and a real go-getter. Blond and bouncy, she was grateful to have a job that put her sociology degree to good use, and Kat was happy to have her organizational and fund-raising skills for StrongGirls.

"*Who* was *that?*"

"The fireman who saved our lives," Kat said, trying to sound casual.

"Is he cute?"

"Well…yeah. Not cute, exactly. Really handsome, but not movie-star pretty."

"I figured he had *something* going for him."

"Why do you say that?"

"Because of how you sounded when you talked to him. Your voice got all mushy."

"It did not!" Kat laughed. "You have a lot of imagination. I am grateful to this man. I admire the fact that he risks his life for strangers. That's all."

"Hmm, we'll see." Deb looked at the newspaper classifieds spread out over her coffee table. "How goes the apartment hunt? And no, I'm not anxious for you to leave. Take as long as you want."

"Dismal. The rental market is tight right now, especially in my price range. I looked at a couple yesterday, but…" She shuddered. *Grim* was the only word that fit.

Her budget had been tight the past few months. She'd obtained the funding to start StrongGirls and was paying herself a modest salary. But it was less than she'd been making at her previous job as a school counselor, and she'd had to cut a few corners. She'd been lucky that her apartment manager liked her and hadn't raised her rent since she'd moved in. But, she was unlikely to find another apartment that nice for the price she'd been paying.

She would be cutting it close for a while. The settlement from her renters' insurance would help, but it wouldn't cover everything.

She dressed in a flowery skirt and matching blouse from her small stash of new clothes. It was the most feminine outfit of the bunch, the least businesslike, and she chastised herself for "gussying up" for Ethan. Was she trying to impress him? Was that it?

Yes, she was, and unfortunately she knew why.

White-Knight-Syndrome. When one person swooped in and rescued another from a life-or-death situation, the one who'd been rescued sometimes reacted with inappropriate feelings of affection for the rescuer. Sometimes those feelings were mistaken for love. She'd learned about it in one of her many psychology classes, and she'd also experienced the situation in real life.

All right, so it was natural for her to feel a bit gaga over strong, handsome fireman Ethan Basque. That didn't mean she had to act on it. She had enough challenges to occupy her during the coming days and weeks. StrongGirls was expanding into its second phase, and what free time she had needed to be spent with Samantha. She did not have time for a man in her life.

Chapter Three

"What are you doing with that torture device?" Tony was referring to the vacuum cleaner, which Ethan was running over his living room rug. Tony had come over to borrow some wrenches, and he'd stayed to kibitz.

"Cleaning?"

"Why?"

"Because it needs it."

Tony sniffed the air. "I smell furniture polish. And your dishwasher's running, too."

Ethan turned off the vacuum and unplugged it. "Any law against that?"

Tony narrowed his eyes. "You got a girl coming over?"

Was it that obvious? "Kat Holiday is coming over to get her cat," he said casually.

"Aha. I'll get lost, then."

"You don't have to," Ethan said, as he shoved the vacuum into a hall closet.

"But you want me to. You already said you don't think I should hit on her."

True enough. Tony had a way of overwhelming

women—extravagant dinners, flowers, gifts, lavish compliments. All of it sincere.

He could fall head over heels for a woman in ten minutes. But his romances always burned hot and quick, then fizzled. Usually, the woman got tired of Tony's devotion and dumped him, causing lots of despair and teeth-gnashing—until the next woman came along. And there was always another one.

Ethan didn't want Kat to be just another of his friend's conquests in a long line of them.

"The wrenches are with my other tools in the garage. You remember where the key is."

Tony gave him a knowing look and sauntered toward the kitchen and out the back door.

Maybe Ethan would ask Kat out. Just a friendly low-key date. They could go to a ball game and include Samantha—if the child got over being terrified of him. That was something else he needed to worry about.

The doorbell rang at exactly ten. Not wanting to appear overeager, Ethan took his time getting to the door, Bashira draped over his shoulder. The kitten—who turned out to be orange, once the soot had been washed off—had spent a good deal of his time riding on Ethan's shoulder.

Ethan schooled his face, then opened the door, and there she was, looking fifty times better than he'd imagined. She wore a short skirt, revealing spectacular, bare tan legs, and a wispy blouse with flowers that chased themselves across her breasts. Her abundant, chocolate-brown hair had been rolled into a loose coil atop her head, but several wild curls had escaped to frame her round, soft face, which reminded him of one of those Renaissance portraits of the Madonna.

She smiled when she saw him, but her gaze was on the kitten. "Bashira! Aren't you making yourself comfortable."

Ethan opened the door wider to let her inside. "He's a handful. Gets into trouble, if you don't watch him every minute."

"Don't I know it? Cat-proofing my apartment was more trouble than child-proofing." She held out her hands, and Ethan transferred the kitten to her. She cuddled Bashira against her cheek, cooing softly. "Oh, your poor little kitty ears. You must have been so hurt and scared." She looked up at Ethan, her big brown eyes suspiciously shiny, and he felt his knees wobble. "I can't thank you enough for taking the trouble to rescue him. Samantha will be so happy to see him again."

"Tony is really the one who rescued him." Ethan didn't want to remind Kat of Tony, but he believed in giving credit where it was due. "Where is Samantha? Is she doing okay?"

"She's with her father this weekend, while I deal with stuff," she said brightly, but then her smile faded slightly. "You can't imagine how much there is to do."

"You have five minutes for a cup of coffee, though, right? I just put on a fresh pot."

She looked tempted for the moment, but then she shook her head. "I've got to find a new apartment. You'd think it wouldn't be that hard, but every place I've looked at is either too expensive, won't take pets or it's just…yuck." She bit her full lower lip and buried her face in the kitten's fur.

He could tell she was struggling with her emotions. Ethan's mind raced. He had a vacant apartment. It was small and it still needed some work, but it was livable. "I have an idea."

Five minutes later, Kat was walking around the one-bedroom apartment above his garage, checking out the single closet.

"Not that I have much to put *in* the closet," she said with a laugh.

"I know it's probably smaller than you want," Ethan said. "And the kitchen is awful. But I'm putting in new cabinets and appliances."

"It's really not so bad," she said. "So how much rent would you charge?"

He shrugged. "It was just sitting here empty. You don't have to pay me rent."

"What? Of course I do." She looked at him like he was a little bit crazy. And maybe he was. Any normal person would charge rent. But he couldn't see himself taking money out of Kat's pocket, not when she'd just lost everything in a fire.

"Tell you what," Ethan said. "I'll charge you rent. But you don't have to pay me now. You're going to need money for a lot of stuff. We can defer it until you're back on your feet."

"That's very generous of you. But I make it a policy never to go into debt. It's something I counsel my girls on, over and over."

"Your girls?" She had more than one?

"The StrongGirls. It's a program I'm running for teenage girls. I try to teach them to become independent and take responsibility for their lives. We do group and individual counseling, life-skills coaching, relationship coaching, help them with job applications, encourage teamwork and networking and goal-setting—a little bit of everything."

Ethan was impressed. He figured she did *something* for a living, but he hadn't imagined that. "You're running the whole program?"

"Well, that sounds more impressive than it is. I came up with the concept and curriculum, and I got the grant that allowed me to start it up. But it's a fledgling program. I only have four groups of girls, two employees and a tiny storefront office. But it's going really well, so far. Zero pregnancies, zero dropouts—" She stopped herself. "I am so sorry. I've been living and breathing this program for more than a year and I drone on and on about it at the slightest encouragement."

"Hey, don't apologize. It sounds like you're doing something great." Great, but she probably wasn't making a lot of money. "Really, you don't have to pay me rent."

She shook her head. "I couldn't look my girls in the eye if I accepted charity from you, when I'm perfectly able to handle this. That's what being a StrongGirl is all about." She pulled her checkbook from her purse. "So how much is the rent?"

"You're taking the apartment?"

"Yes. I love this neighborhood. I've wanted to live here since I first moved to Oak Cliff."

Ethan reluctantly named a figure. It was less than he could probably get on the open market, but not so low that Kat would think he was giving her charity. He hadn't realized she would be so touchy about someone trying to help her out.

She wrote out the check for the first month's rent and handed it to him. "You should also be charging me a security deposit and a pet deposit, you know."

"I trust you."

She looked at him, perplexed. "You don't even know me."

"I'm a good judge of character. Anyway, we'll soon know each other better." Maybe a lot better.

Her eyes widened slightly, as if she'd read his thoughts. Their gazes held for a long moment. He could almost see the sparks flying between them.

Unable to bear the tension a moment longer without touching her, he broke the silence. "So, when do you want to move in? I work tomorrow—twenty-four on, forty-eight off. But any 'off' day I can help you."

She waved away his offer. "I only have a few things. I can manage."

Right. She had lost all of her belongings. "What about furniture?"

"I'll get it worked out," she said breezily. "One step at a time."

"Bashira can stay with me until you get settled in the apartment. No sense moving him twice."

"Are you sure?"

"Sure, I'm sure."

She stood on her toes and gave him a quick kiss on the cheek. "Thank you, again. You're a lifesaver in more ways than one."

From his front door, he watched the way her skirt hugged her rounded hips as she made her way to her beat-up compact car. His face tingled where her lips had touched it. It was such an innocent kiss, barely a peck, but it had electrified every nerve.

He hoped he was doing the right thing, having Kat so close. He liked her. He wanted to get to know her better. He could see that something might develop between them. But if things didn't work out, her proximity could get uncomfortable in a hurry.

KAT SPENT the rest of the day power shopping. It was Saturday, and every store was packed. She moved through Wal-Mart like a tornado, filling her cart with everything from sneakers to toothpaste to cleaning products. Then it was on to a discount furniture store to buy a futon and bed frame, as well as a twin mattress and springs. She was determined to get Samantha the canopy bed she wanted, but there wasn't time today to track one down. It was when she tried to buy a small table and chairs that her credit card maxed out.

She'd never had a credit card refused in her life. But she'd never charged thousands of dollars of medical care to Visa, either. She would be able to pay off the card, or at least a good chunk of it, when her insurance came through, but that wouldn't be until next week at the earliest.

With a sigh she took out the book of temporary checks she'd gotten from the bank, looked at the balance and decided the table would have to wait.

At least she had the use of a pickup truck. Deb had been kind enough to trade cars with Kat.

It was almost dark by the time Kat pulled into her new driveway with her belongings. Her plan was to bring the cleaning supplies in first and give the apartment a good scrubbing. It obviously had sat vacant a long time and looked it. But the first thing she noticed when she opened the gate into the backyard were the lights blazing in her new place.

Curious, she climbed the stairs. As she neared the door, she heard voices and laughter coming from inside.

She knocked, feeling a bit ridiculous since this was her own apartment. Ethan opened the door with a big grin. "Kat. Welcome home."

Ethan and two other people stood in her living room, watching her expectantly. One of the others was Tony Veracruz, the paramedic who had transported Samantha and Kat to the hospital. He gave her a megawatt smile and a two-finger salute. The woman, she soon learned, was Priscilla Garner, another firefighter who'd fought her apartment fire.

"So, what are you all doing here?" Kat asked. But the answer was evident. She saw brooms, a mop, a bucket, various rags and a bottle of Murphy's oil soap, and the air was full of cleaning smells.

"I couldn't let you move in with the place such a mess," Ethan said.

"And he drafted us to help," Priscilla added.

"This is so nice," Kat said, giving Ethan a reproving look, "but you didn't have to. You're already doing me such a huge favor letting me live here."

"It's no big deal," Ethan said.

"I was going to do the cleaning." She pointed to the broom and mop and cleaning products she'd brought. "But thanks."

Ever since her divorce, when she'd realized how much she had allowed Chuck to do for her without giving as much in return, she'd felt uncomfortable whenever anyone did her a favor. If someone donated time or money or materials to the StrongGirls program, that was one thing. But to her personally... Well, it brought up all kinds of feelings, inadequacy being the major one.

Did Ethan think that just because she'd been through a fire, she wasn't capable of cleaning her own apartment?

She and Virginia Wilmington, her staff psychologist, had talked at length about this issue of Kat's, and she knew her feelings were exaggerated and not entirely logical. But it was a knee-jerk response.

She stifled it. "How about I spring for dinner, then?" she suggested brightly. "Pizza?" She could afford that, at least.

"Pizza's always good," Ethan said. "But no way are you paying. I wouldn't feel right about that."

Why not? she wondered. "You're not one of those

chauvinists who thinks women ought not to pay for anything, are you?"

Priscilla laughed. "Honey, you're talking to a male firefighter. They're all chauvinists."

"Hey," Tony objected as he wiped off the last of the grime from a window. "Would a chauvinist clean windows? Anyway, we stick up for you at the station."

"You guys are the most enlightened of the bunch," she agreed. "But that is *so* not saying much."

"Where is your furniture?" Ethan asked Kat. "We'll help you move in."

"It's out in my truck." She nodded in the general direction of the driveway. "But it's just a few things, and I can move…" She didn't get a chance to finish. The men were out the door.

Priscilla shrugged. "Testosterone."

"They really don't have to do this," Kat said. She hated being reduced to a clichéd helpless female. But Ethan commandeered the transfer of items from the truck to the apartment and he wouldn't let her touch anything heavy.

It didn't take long. She hadn't been kidding when she said she didn't have much furniture—just the twin bed, the futon and a cute little coffee table, marked way down because it had a scratch.

"Is this all?" Ethan asked, studying the results with a doubtful eye.

Okay, it did look bare. But that would change once she got her insurance. "It's all for now. I didn't have time to get more than a few essentials. I'll go shopping next week."

"You don't even have a table," Ethan objected. "Where are you going to eat?"

"I can sit on the floor in front of the coffee table." She'd certainly taken meals in stranger places. Like when she was a little girl, standing outside the door of her apartment, eating chili right out of the can while her mother was inside, doing whatever with her latest boyfriend.

"Kat," Priscilla said, "I'd love to stay for pizza, but I have a racquetball game in twenty minutes." She nudged Tony.

"Oh, right. I have to go, too," he said. "But let us know if you need anything."

Kat thanked them both again, and they cleared out.

"Guess it's just you and me," Ethan said. "I have a coupon for Home Run Pizza."

Kat was starving. She might not have a table, but Ethan did. The idea of relaxing, putting her feet up and shooting the breeze with sexy Ethan Basque had a certain appeal. But just then her cell phone rang. Kat saw that it was Chuck's number and she answered immediately.

"Mommy?" Samantha's tone was uncharacteristically timid. "Can you come get me?"

"Is something wrong?" Kat's heart rate accelerated.

"No, I just want you to come. I miss you."

Normally, Samantha loved weekends with her father. She adored her baby half sister and liked helping take care of her. "I miss you too, sweetie. Can I talk to your dad, please?"

Chuck reported that Sam had been fretful all day, so they agreed to end the weekend visit early just this once. "Tell her I'll be there in a few minutes."

Ethan puttered around while Kat talked on the phone, but she knew he'd heard.

"Samantha needs me," Kat explained, her voice tinged with regret.

"Any reason we couldn't all have pizza?"

Kat shook her head. "I'm sorry, Ethan. I hope Sam won't still be afraid of you, but I don't know. And frankly, I'm not up to dealing with another bout of tears or hysteria tonight."

"I understand. Promise you'll ask if you need anything."

"I promise." But he'd already done so much. How could she accept even more? She'd fought hard for her independence, and now she was teaching her Strong-Girls to do the same. She wanted them to be able to rely on themselves when they reached adulthood—not on the government, not on alcohol or drugs, and not on a man.

She'd set herself up as a role model. The way she coped with this detour in her life would provide a good example—*if* she handled things right. If she stayed strong.

Ethan took both her hands in his and gave them an encouraging squeeze. But then he drew her closer. And the way he was looking at her, she knew he wanted to kiss her. The knowledge sent a thrilling shiver up her back.

She'd opened that door by giving him an impulsive kiss on the cheek earlier today, so she shouldn't be surprised. But she was, a little. After her grueling day, without even one look in a mirror, she was hardly a glamour girl, and the idea that he was apparently attracted to her was unsettling. Not unpleasant, just unsettling.

But she was too tired to think about whether it was good or bad, these budding feelings between her and her handsome rescuer. It was just a kiss.

He must have sensed her acquiescence, because he moved in closer. Then his mouth was on hers, warm, welcoming. Their arms slid around each other as the kiss deepened, and Kat tipped her head back, going with the feeling, surrendering to it.

It felt good. It felt different than any kiss she'd ever experienced, though she couldn't have said why.

For a few seconds, anyway, she forgot about everything else and just let herself enjoy feeling one hundred percent desirable female. She gave herself over to the sensations, the smell of his skin, the feel of the strong muscles in his back against her open palms.

He could have pressed his advantage, but he didn't. He withdrew slowly, ending the embrace with a light kiss to her forehead. "I'll hold you to that promise."

Later, as she drove to North Dallas to pick up Sam, she wondered exactly what she *had* promised. She couldn't remember.

Chapter Four

It was after dark by the time Kat and Samantha entered their apartment with two large bags of toys and clothes. Chuck had calmly loaded Kat's car with all the personal belongings Samantha kept at his house—clothes, toys, hair ribbons and even a beanbag chair. She would need some familiar things around her, he'd explained.

Samantha dropped the lighter bag she carried and sniffed disapprovingly. "It smells funny."

"It's just cleaning stuff," Kat said. "And look, look who's here to greet you!" Bashira came trotting out of the bedroom and straight to Samantha, meowing plaintively. Ethan must have brought over the kitten while she was gone. Kat appreciated his thoughtfulness, especially when she herself had forgotten about the kitten.

Samantha and Bashira had been inseparable before the fire. But to Kat's surprise, Samantha barely looked at the kitten and made no move to pet him or pick him up. She walked past him, through the combination living/dining room and into the bedroom. Then she turned back, her mouth set mulishly.

"Mommy, I don't like this place."

"It needs work," Kat agreed in a light tone. "But we'll get it fixed up. Anyway, it's just temporary, until we can find some place that's a little bigger." She carried an armload of Samantha's clothes toward the bedroom, then realized she had no coat hangers. Every time she turned around, she discovered something else she needed to buy.

"Is this my room?" Samantha asked, shadowing Kat.

"Yup. There's a big pecan tree right outside your window."

The child was unimpressed. "Where's your room?"

"I'll sleep in the other room."

"I want you to sleep in here."

"Hmm, it's an awfully small bed for two people."

"I don't care."

Kat ruffled Samantha's wavy brown hair, so like her own. Looking at her daughter was sometimes like looking in a mirror from twenty years ago. "All right, I guess for the first night that's okay. But you'll like this place once you get used to it. In fact, there's a little girl who lives right next door, who's about your age. Well, a little older, but I bet she would play with you."

A spark of interest flared in Samantha's eyes. "What's her name?"

"Her name's Jasmine. I think she goes to your school."

"Jasmine Veracruz?" Samantha was definitely interested.

"Yes, that's her name. Do you know her?"

"She's a third-grader." Samantha said this as if being a third-grader was the most exalted position in the world.

"We'll ask her over to play soon, okay?"

"Okay." Samantha sat on the bed, bouncing slightly. "I wish I had my bunny quilt."

Kat could see Sam was close to tears, and her own throat felt tight. She sat down next to Sam and put her arm around her. "It's hard, losing all our stuff. But try to remember, Sam, that what we lost are just things. Things can be replaced. What's important is that we're both alive and we weren't hurt. The firemen did a good job getting everybody out of the building."

Sam said nothing.

"Hey, I've got an idea. At the grocery store today I bought brownie mix. Why don't we try out our new oven and bake some brownies?"

Samantha brightened slightly. "Okay."

"We can make two pans. And in the morning we can take one of them to the fire station, to thank the firefighters who rescued us."

Kat was pleased that Samantha didn't immediately oppose the idea. She did seem to be thinking it over, though. "Is that where they have the fire trucks?"

"Yes, and all the firefighters live there. They cook and eat and sleep in that house, like a family, just waiting for a fire to happen, so they can rush over as fast as they can and put it out." At least, she thought that was how it worked. Frankly, she didn't know much about firefighting. She would benefit from a tour of the station, too. "They're very brave people, and I think it's important that we show how much we appreciate what they do. Okay? Is it a plan?"

"Okay," she said without much enthusiasm.

ETHAN HAD BEEN WATCHING his apartment—Kat's apartment—off and on all evening and he was starting to feel like a voyeur. His heart pounded every time he thought about that kiss, about how warm and pliant Kat had felt in his arms, and how much he'd wanted to do more than kiss her. He was frustrated beyond measure that he couldn't go over there now.

Earlier, Tony had said something about a darts tournament at Brady's. He decided to head over and see what was going on. It had to be better than sitting around here, feeling antsy.

Brady's Tavern had been across the street from Fire Station 59 for as long as anyone could remember. It had withstood Prohibition, the Great Depression and Oak Cliff's ever-changing liquor laws. The neon signs were always about ten years out of date—currently the one over the bar, next to the naked lady painting, depicted the Budweiser frogs.

During all those years, Brady's had been the place for Oak Cliff cops and firefighters to hang out after hours. The two groups were often at odds, but for some reason at Brady's they all got along. The cops talked about their cases, while shooting darts; the firefighters talked about great fires from their fathers' era, while they played shuffleboard.

They bought drinks for the women—"siren sisters"—who hung out at Brady's strictly to meet cops and firefighters.

Ethan wasn't much of a barfly, but Captain Campeon had not-so-subtly indicated that a little off-shift camaraderie at Brady's might help the rookies bond with their more seasoned brethren.

The place was hopping this Saturday night. A few heads turned to look as Ethan entered, but no one greeted him. He wasn't a regular, not yet, and only a few of the faces were vaguely familiar.

Then he saw Bing Tate. He waved a greeting, but Bing pointedly turned away as if he hadn't seen.

Well, hell, he wasn't going to let Tate ruin his mood. He'd kissed Kat Holiday, and nothing was going to detract from that.

Finally, he spotted Priscilla, sitting at a high table by herself, nursing a glass of wine. She was watching the shuffleboard table, as if it were the final round of the world championships.

Ethan got himself a beer and crossed the sticky plank floor to join her. "What's up?"

She jumped, startled—obviously having missed his arrival. "Oh, hi. Nothing. Tony and I both got eliminated from darts during the first round." Her gaze drifted back toward the shuffleboard game. "I nearly hit one of the spectators with my first throw. Tony went home, but I wanted to finish my wine. What are you doing here? I thought you'd be with Kat."

"The pizza thing didn't work out. Is the shuffleboard that interesting?" He only recognized one of the players. His name was Roark Epperson, and he was an instructor at the fire school. He was also one of the top arson investigators in the country and the lead on investigating the warehouse fire that had killed three of their own.

Priscilla's head snapped back. "No, but due to a distinct lack of anything else interesting going on, shuffleboard won my attention."

Ethan took a drink from his mug. "So Captain Campeon's plan to build camaraderie isn't exactly working, huh?"

Before she could answer, an obviously inebriated man sidled up to the table. "Hey, babe, wanna rematch? Jus' you and me?" He leered at her. "Dartboard's free."

"Um, no, thanks."

"Well, then, be that way, Ice Princess." He turned and staggered away.

Otis Granger, who happened to be on his way to the bar, overheard the last comment. "Prissy, did he just call you Ice Princess?"

"Yeah. What about it?"

Otis laughed. "I like it. Ice Princess." And he laughed the rest of the way to the bar.

Ethan couldn't help but like Otis. He was cheerful and had an easy laugh, and he'd been one of the first to start to thaw toward the rookies. But he did enjoy tormenting Priscilla.

Priscilla sighed. "If this is camaraderie, I can live without it."

THE DIRTIEST JOB at Fire Station 59 was cleaning the bathroom. Once again, Ethan had drawn the short stick, but he accepted the chore stoically, as he did whatever task he was given. Such was the lot of a rookie.

Tony was off the hook for chores today, since he had to study for a test in order to keep his paramedic certification current, but Priscilla hadn't fared much better than Ethan. She had to mop the floors. She wielded the mop as if it were the handle of a butter churn. Sometimes he had a hard time believing anyone could be as ignorant of housekeeping skills as Priscilla was. But it wasn't something she'd had much practice with. She'd grown up in a Highland Park mansion, with multiple servants, and though she tried to shake off her upper-crust background, sometimes it showed.

"Those ladies on the TV commercials always make mopping look so easy," Priscilla grumbled, as she bounced her mop across the gray bathroom tiles.

Ethan agreed. Likewise, mildew did not disappear with one swipe of the sponge. He had to put a brush and some muscle into it.

"Visitors on the premises!" someone yelled, a leftover practice from the days when a firefighter— and they were males only in those days—might walk nude from the showers to his bunk or zone out in front of a skin flick. With women firefighters in the picture, no one did that anymore. Not much, anyway. Some of the old-timers deeply resented the loss of freedom, but Ethan didn't see what the big deal was.

The visitor could have been anyone, from a chief

making a surprise inspection to a wife dropping off a set of keys or a cell phone to a forgetful husband. Ethan was only slightly curious, and he figured if it concerned him Captain Campeon would call him.

The captain wasn't shy about that sort of thing.

Then he heard the word "brownies" mentioned, and he dropped his scrub brush and washed his hands. If a family member or a nice neighbor had baked brownies for the fire station, he wanted in on it. If he waited even five minutes, they'd be gone.

Priscilla shook her head as she squeezed her mop head, getting more water down the leg of her navy blue pants than into the bucket. "You guys are so predictable. Mention brownies and your brain short-circuits. The only thing worse is mentioning breasts."

"Breasts?" Ethan looked around. "Where?"

Priscilla flicked him with mop water as he passed. "Hey, bring me a brownie, will you?"

"If there's an extra." He headed for the dining hall, where a half dozen of his comrades were already gathered as someone wielded a knife over a pan of brownies.

Standing off to the side was Kat.

Ethan froze in the doorway and drank in the sight of the woman who'd invaded his dreams the night before. She had Samantha with her, clinging like a newborn monkey, hiding her face against Kat's pink T-shirt.

Ethan couldn't really blame her. The feeding frenzy unfolding before her eyes was enough to frighten a grizzly bear.

He stepped into the room and cleared his throat.

Conversation stopped and Kat fixed her eyes on him, her full lips slightly open. The other guys, who apparently knew these were the two Ethan had helped to rescue, waited to see what she'd say.

"We brought brownies."

"I see."

"We wanted to thank you—all of you," she added hastily, blushing.

Ethan was charmed by her shyness. She obviously didn't want anyone to think she was singling Ethan out for special treatment. The guys parted like the Red Sea, as he approached. "Hi, Kat. Samantha, is that you? I can't tell with you hiding your face."

His cajoling had no effect, except to make the little girl clutch at her mother's shirt even more. Her knuckles were white.

"We really appreciate sweets," he continued awkwardly. "Especially chocolate." He looked down at the pan.

Empty.

Kat looked, too. "I guess I should have brought two pans."

With guilty mumbles everyone else ambled out of the dining hall, making excuses about work to do. Soon it was just Ethan, Kat and Samantha, who still hid her face.

"Did you get a brownie, Samantha?" Ethan asked.

"Samantha," Kat urged, when her daughter didn't respond, "Mr. Basque is talking to you. Think maybe you could answer him?"

"I don't like brownies," Samantha answered, her

voice muffled. She refused to turn her face away from her mother. "Mommy, can we go now?"

Not a great start, but at least she wasn't screaming.

"Don't you want to take a tour of the fire station?" Kat asked. "Captain Campeon said he would show us around. I bet he would let you sit in the fire truck."

That was a bit of a surprise to Ethan. Eric Campeon, still finding his footing as a newly minted captain with his first command, had made it clear he didn't like civilians hanging out at the station. But then, Campeon didn't like much of anything. The guy never smiled. Ethan had a hard time picturing Campeon catering to a mom and her little girl.

But apparently he would never get the chance to see it, because Samantha was having none of it. "I just want to *go,*" she said, sounding more agitated.

Ethan searched for something to say, anything to ease the little girl's discomfort. Finally, inspiration struck. "Do you like puppies, Samantha?"

"No."

"Oh, she does so like puppies," Kat said impatiently. "She's just being contrary."

"We have some puppies out back. Daisy, our mascot, had a litter." Apparently Daisy had once had free run of the place, despite a "no dogs" rule enacted by the department a few years ago. But Campeon had put an end to that when he'd taken over. That was just before Ethan had been assigned to work at Station 59.

Samantha had no response to the puppy suggestion, but at least she didn't reject it outright.

"They're Dalmatian puppies," Ethan added. "You've seen *101 Dalmatians,* right?"

"Only about fifty times," Kat said. "Come on, Samantha. Let's go look at the puppies."

Samantha allowed herself to be led out of the kitchen, down a hallway and out a back door to a small fenced yard. Inside the yard was a spacious dog run, with a concrete floor and an insulated shelter and misters to keep Daisy cool during the hot months. The guys had spared no effort or expense in giving Daisy the best quarters possible, once she'd been banished outside.

Inside the run, spotted puppies were everywhere. They were about five weeks old now, at that cute stage where they were galumphing around with too-big clumsy puppy feet, curious about everything. Ethan opened the door to the run and they poured out into the yard—and straight for Samantha.

Samantha climbed Kat like a tree. "Mommy!" she shrieked with alarm, as Kat picked her up. Samantha was small for her age, probably no more than forty pounds.

"Samantha, honey, they won't hurt you."

Ethan, realizing he'd made a tactical error in letting them all out at once, hastily herded them back to their anxious mother, leaving just one outside the run. He scooped up the little female and held her out for Samantha to see.

"How about we visit with just one at a time?"

Despite her fright, Samantha did appear interested. Kat put her down, and she sat on the grass as Ethan set the puppy down close to her. Puppy and child eyed each other suspiciously. Then the puppy toddled close, and Samantha reached out to pet it. With the slightest encouragement, the puppy was all over the little girl. Ethan watched as Kat sighed with relief.

The two of them retreated to a picnic table. Ethan, Tony and Priscilla sometimes took their meals out here, when the tension inside the firehouse got a bit thick.

"Who does she belong to?" Kat asked. "Daisy, I mean."

"All of us, I guess. She used to belong to John Simon." He waited to see if she recognized the name.

Kat nodded. "One of the men killed in the warehouse fire. I read about it in the paper. What a terrible tragedy. He was from this station?"

"All three were. John Simon, David Latier and Lamar Burkins." He spoke their names like an invocation. They were imprinted on his brain as deeply as they would be on the new firefighters' memorial the city was planning.

Kat's eyes dropped, and she shook her head as if she couldn't even stand to think about it. After her recent brush with death, he wasn't surprised. "That must have been awful for you guys. I'm so sorry."

"It happened before I was assigned here," Ethan said. "Tony, Priscilla and I filled the vacancies." Which was a bit unusual. Normally, three rookies wouldn't be assigned to the same station. But no experienced firefighters wanted to be transferred here. Firefighters were a superstitious lot. And when the old captain had retired after the tragedy and word got around that Eric Campeon was to assume his position, the department couldn't get anyone with experience to move there voluntarily.

The deaths had rocked the firefighting community to the core. Ethan would never forget the day he'd learned of the tragedy. He'd still been in training, and classes had been called off for the rest of the day. One of his fellow trainees had been so unnerved by the event that he'd quit. It had been years since a firefighter had been killed in the line of duty in Dallas. Three at one time—it was almost too much to take in.

"Did they catch the arsonist?" Kat asked.

Ethan shook his head. "Roark Epperson, the lead arson investigator, is still looking into it. It's not the arsonist's first fire. He's been at it for close to a year now, and his fires are getting more and more ambitious."

They lapsed into silence briefly, watching Samantha play with the puppy. The little girl had lost the tight, wary look on her face, and she actually smiled when the puppy pounced on a ball.

"That's a sight I haven't seen lately," Kat said. "A smile."

"She's not bouncing back?"

"That timid, sullen, terrified little girl is radically different from the Samantha I thought I knew. She seems to be afraid of everything, but mostly of having another fire. I just don't know what—" She cut herself off as her voice choked with tears. "I'm sorry. You don't need to hear about this."

"Yes, I do." Ethan couldn't help himself. He reached out and brushed a tear away with the pad of his finger. "I'd like to help."

"You can't take on the responsibility for every person you help in a fire," Kat said. "You'd be spreading yourself pretty thin."

"Let me worry about how thin I spread myself. What about if I do a safety inspection of your new digs? We can make a game of it. We can appoint Samantha as your official fire safety marshal. I think we have toy badges and hats for that sort of thing—I can check."

Kat hesitated. "I'm not sure that's a good idea. What if talking about fire makes it worse? Last night, she was so afraid she made me sleep with her."

"The more she understands about what causes fires and how to prevent them, the more secure she'll feel." Ethan knew that firsthand. He'd previously worked in construction. At one job site, he'd been up on a high floor of a skyscraper installing drywall, when suddenly smoke had engulfed his work area. He'd been forced to grope his way to a stairwell, scared out of his mind. He'd never wanted to be that frightened again, and that was what had first given him the idea of joining the fire department. Know the enemy.

"That's what my staff psychologist said, too." Kat drew a deep breath in and sighed, gathering control of her emotions.

There were no more tears, for which Ethan was extremely grateful. He could face a wall of flame, a room of smoke and fierce temperatures. But not a crying female, not when he didn't know how to help.

The door banged open and Captain Campeon appeared, looking like a thunderstorm personified. "Basque, what the *hell* are you doing out here?"

"Showing our guest some hospitality, sir," Ethan answered without hesitation. One thing he'd learned about the captain—he hated timidity or any show of weakness.

"Put that dog back where it belongs. Don't you have work to do?"

"Yes, sir," Ethan said, throwing a wink toward Kat, who'd started moving toward Samantha the moment Campeon had appeared. Samantha looked toward her mother, her face tight again, obviously not liking the raised voice.

"Sorry, this is my fault," Kat said, taking Samantha's hand while Ethan grabbed the pup and returned it to its mother. "I didn't mean to keep anyone from his job. I know you all have important work to do."

Oh, yeah, scrubbing grout was a real public-safety must-do. Ethan wanted to argue that nothing was her fault, that Campeon was being his usual stiff-necked jerk. But firefighters who valued their careers didn't argue with their captains in front of civilians—or at any other time, for that matter.

"I'll walk you back to your car," Ethan said. He wanted just another minute or two with Kat, minus the captain staring down his nose at them.

Campeon stepped forward. "Would you still like that tour of the fire station?" he asked grudgingly.

Kat looked down at Samantha, who shook her head. "I think maybe we'll save that for another day."

Campeon nodded his understanding.

"My car's right there," Kat said to Ethan, pointing toward the parking lot. "You don't have to walk us. But Ethan…?"

"Yes?"

"Maybe the safety inspection is a good idea."

He nodded, suddenly tongue-tied, with Campeon staring poison darts at him. Then Kat and Samantha were gone.

All right, then. He was making headway. Samantha still looked at him as if he were the Creature from the Black Lagoon and refused to talk to him, but at least she hadn't gone into a screaming panic when she saw him this time.

Feeling pretty good, as if he could tackle all the mildew in a small tropical country, Ethan reentered the common room—only to be greeted by an ugly mob.

"Ohhh, Ethan," Otis Granger trilled in his best falsetto. He'd put a string mop over his head. "Will you show me your big fireman muscles?" He batted his eyelashes and pretended to swoon.

"Ohhh, Ethan," Jim Peterson said, attempting a breathy Marilyn Monroe imitation. "I just love the way you swing that hose!" At this, four or five other guys fell into hopeless hysterics.

"All right, you guys, break it up. I just wanted to show

the little girl Daisy's pups, okay?" He endured a few more catcalls and off-color comments before facing a really scary proposition—Priscilla, in chocolate withdrawal.

She stood blocking his way into the bathroom hallway. "Where's my brownie?"

"I didn't get one, either. Talk to those piranhas in there. They're the ones who reduced a pan of brownies to crumbs in less than thirty seconds."

"And they was damn good, too," someone taunted.

"Crumbs? We left crumbs? I don't think so," another firefighter added.

"I'd rescue a woman every day of my life, if she'd bake for me," Otis called out. "But not you, Prissy. We know you wouldn't bake."

"Naw, she'd hire someone to bake for her."

Priscilla yelled out a good-natured obscenity, after which things died down and everyone returned to their tasks.

"Why do they have to be such jerks?" Priscilla wondered aloud as she resumed her ineffective mopping.

Ethan actually laughed. "Count your blessings, Pris. Last week they were ignoring us, looking right through us. This week they're harassing us. I think it's a step up."

Chapter Five

Ethan and Tony were clearing the lunch dishes when Bing Tate entered with a bookish young woman dressed in khakis and carrying a tape recorder. "Got a young lady of the press here, wants to talk to the *hero,*" Tate announced.

Aw, hell.

Tony nudged him. "That would be you."

"I don't want to talk to a reporter," he whispered. But it was too late. The reporter rushed up to him, eyes wide. "Are you the fireman who dragged Kat and Samantha Holiday from a burning building?"

"Lieutenant Murphy McCrae is the one you should talk to," Ethan said, drying his hands on a dish towel. "He was in charge of the search-and-rescue."

"But you did rush into a burning building and carry out an unconscious woman and her child?"

"A lot of us were in that building."

"But you did the rescuing?" she persisted.

"Look, I'm just a rookie. I was doing my job. You'll have to talk to my captain if you want to do an interview. It's policy," he said apologetically.

"Aw, don't go all modest on us now," Tate said. "You're the hero, the man of the hour. His first fire, and he turns into Superman." Ethan might have taken it in the same vein as the earlier teasing—as good-natured ribbing. But there was nothing good-natured in the tone of Tate's voice.

"It was your first fire ever?" the woman asked, shoving the tape recorder in his face. She was oblivious to the undercurrents.

"Look, why don't you talk to the captain?" Ethan suggested again. "I can take you to his office."

"Ethan just started two weeks ago," Bing said. "That's Ethan Basque. E-T-H—"

Fortunately, just then the alarm sounded.

"Excuse us," Ethan said brusquely, hoping the reporter would be gone when he got back from his run. Firefighters weren't allowed to talk to the press without prior approval. Bing knew that, and he'd deliberately tried to get Ethan in trouble.

That day, Tate was on paramedic duty, while Tony rode the truck with Ethan. It wasn't ideal, two rookies in the same unit. But no amount of shuffling personnel prevented it from happening sometimes.

As the engine and truck rolled out, details of the emergency filtered in. A young child had dialed 9-1-1, reporting that his mother had fallen and something was burning. Potentially, a disaster. When they arrived at the small house, at the end of a row of abandoned houses in a blighted neighborhood, they found three tearful children standing in the front yard of a humble frame house. One of them pointed to the house and rattled off rapid Spanish.

Everyone looked at Tony. Most of them understood some Spanish, including Ethan. But not when it was spoken that quickly. Tony, however, was fluent.

"He says his mother's inside and she fell," Tony translated.

Four firefighters tried to get through the front door at the same time. Inside, the house was smoky, and the source was quickly found—a pot on the stove. McCrae stepped forward matter-of-factly and put it out with an extinguisher.

Tony and Ethan located the woman—lying on the floor, nine months pregnant if she was a day, screaming incoherently.

They knelt down beside her and Tony conversed with her for a bit, calming her as he did. Ethan couldn't understand the words, but he recognized what was going on. The woman was in hard labor.

Tate and his partner, Kevin Sinclair, were right behind Tony and Ethan with the gurney. Tony stood aside.

"What's she saying?" Ethan asked.

"She says she's having the baby. Like, right this second."

And sure enough, she was. Before they could even transfer her to the stretcher, the baby crowned.

"Oh, boy," said Tate. "It's gonna be one of those days." And with eight firefighters gaping, the woman swiftly gave birth.

Ethan, shocked at how fast it happened, had to hand

it to Tate, who handled the situation well. "You rookies pay attention," McCrae said with a laugh. "You'll have to do this soon enough."

Ethan had never seen a baby being born before. It was awe-inspiring. He thought about how it would be when he had a wife and they had kids. Not if, but when. He'd always known he would get married and have kids someday. The prospect hadn't ever felt so terrifying. It would be awful watching someone he loved in that much pain, unable to help.

The ambulance took off, with mother and baby apparently fine. Ladder truck 59 stayed behind with the children until a couple of police cruisers were able to pick them up and figure out where they ought to go.

The oldest of the children, a little girl, latched onto Ethan for some reason. "Is my mama okay?" she asked.

"Sure, she's great," Ethan replied, hoping it was true. "And she's gonna bring home a new baby brother."

"Phooey, I wanted a sister. All I got's brothers." And she stomped off.

Tony, who'd been listening to the exchange, laughed. "Ever the charmer, Basque."

"Yeah, I'm batting a thousand with the little ones."

"Speaking of which, how're things going with Kat—really? And who paid for the pizza?"

"We didn't have pizza. She had to pick up Samantha, which meant I had to get lost."

"The kid really doesn't like you?"

"Looks that way."

"Well, at least they're living in your backyard. She'll get used to you."

"I don't know. This situation is just temporary, until Kat can get back on her feet and find a better place."

"So make sure her apartment is so nice, she *can't* find a better place. Put in the new kitchen. Paint, wallpaper, install new curtains—do it all."

Ethan had been planning to fix up the apartment anyway, but not all at once. Still, Tony had a point. The nicer he made Kat's living space, the less likely it was that she would want to leave.

And it wasn't just his attraction to Kat that made him want to keep her there. He liked the idea of being able to watch over the two of them. They seemed so alone in the world. Yeah, there was an ex-husband, but where was he when Kat and Sam had been in the hospital?

Ethan understood how hard it was for a single mom. His mother had lost her husband to cancer when Ethan had been just a baby, and she'd never remarried. She'd had little education and no particular job skills, but she'd worked her way up at a soft-drink bottling facility, leaving him with her parents and taking the night shift so she could be home for Ethan during the day. They'd lived in a shabby little neighborhood near an industrial park, but she'd kept their two-bedroom house neat and clean as a church.

Though she was now a senior manager and could afford to live somewhere else, she wouldn't have dreamed of moving. She was the one constant in that shifting community, the one everyone went to for help and advice.

Gloria Basque would approve of Ethan's determination to help Kat and her daughter.

"Do I HAVE TO GO to school?" Samantha asked the following morning, as Kat braided Sam's hair into two long pigtails. "I want to stay with you."

"You know how important school is," Kat explained for the third time. She believed, and Virginia had agreed, that it was important to return Samantha to her regular routine as soon as possible. "And I have to work."

"I could go to the office with you."

"Oh, Samantha. I wish you could. But you already missed one day and you don't want to get behind, do you?"

She sighed. "No. But I think you love the Strong-Girls more than me."

"You know that's not true," Kat said. "I love you more than anyone in the world. We'll do something special together tonight, just us girls."

"Can we get our nails done?" Samantha asked hopefully. A few months earlier, Kat had treated herself to a manicure, and the manicurist had painted Sam's nails, too. Sam had enjoyed the attention.

Manicures weren't really in the budget right now. But maybe Kat could buy some nail polish and they could play beauty shop and do their own nails. "I'll see what I can work out. But right now, we need to hustle if we don't want to be late."

"But I don't want to go to school."

Back at square one. "Sweetie, sometimes we have to do things we don't want to do. That's just part of life."

"But what if our house burns down while I'm gone?"

Ahha. At last Samantha had gotten to what was really bothering her.

"Honey, that isn't very likely." She didn't want to say it was impossible, because it wasn't. "No one around here is going to leave a cigar burning."

"But what if the school burns down?"

Kat hugged her daughter close. "Sam, I know you're scared. But the school has fire alarms and sprinklers and, and…" She couldn't think of anything else. "Can you try not to worry?" She knew darn well that no matter how reassuring she was, Samantha would find something else to worry about.

"I'll try." She grew quiet, staring out the window with that pinched expression that had become habitual since the fire. Finally, she spoke again. "Mommy, what did you mean about the safety 'spection?"

"The— Oh. You mean what I said to Mr. Basque yesterday?"

She nodded.

"Mr. Basque said he would help us do a safety inspection," Kat said carefully, gauging Samantha's reaction. "He's an expert. He'll help us make our new apartment safe, so we don't have to worry."

Samantha looked horrified. "I don't want him to come over."

"Sam, I don't understand," Kat said, with as much patience as she could muster. "Mr. Basque has been very nice to you. He saved your life. He took care of Bashira, even gave him a bath."

"I don't care."

"He let you play with his puppy—and you can't tell me that wasn't fun, because I saw you smiling."

Samantha didn't argue that one, because she knew she'd lose.

Ethan had made Kat smile, too, despite the tears that had been so close to the surface. It was something to do with those brown eyes. He had a tough-looking hard-angled face, not classically handsome but interesting. His nose looked as if it might have been broken once. But those tender, compassionate eyes, such a marked contrast to the rest of him, drew her in and made her feel as if everything would be okay.

She sensed he understood her in a way few others did. Which didn't make a lot of sense, because he didn't know her well, didn't know anything of her harsh upbringing or the fears she harbored for her daughter, growing up in such uncertain times. He knew nothing of the guilt she felt for working such long hours, leaving Samantha in the care of after-school baby-sitters and neighbors far too often. She could have worked at a more traditional job that would have left her more family time and earned her a higher salary.

But StrongGirls was an investment in the future of all girls, including Samantha. If Kat had her way, by the time Samantha was a teenager, the StrongGirl program would be available to every teen girl in the country. It was also an investment in their personal future. As the program grew, Kat would be able to pay herself a better salary.

"I still don't want that man at our house," Samantha said, startling Kat out of her reverie. She'd thought this argument had run its course.

"Can you explain why?" Kat asked.

Sam shrugged, making Kat almost wild with frustration.

"All right, I won't invite him over," Kat said, feeling an out-of-proportion sense of loss. She felt a strong connection with Ethan. She'd even started to believe that they could grow the connection. She hadn't been attracted to a man like this in, well, maybe never. She'd not been a virgin when Chuck had scooped her up, but before Chuck, her experience had been limited to quick, fumbling liaisons with boys who only pretended to care. Boys she'd gone to looking for acceptance, looking for something that would bolster her self-esteem.

Chuck—older and more patient—had shown her that making love could be a pleasant experience. But she'd never felt the body-melting attraction to him that Ethan already ignited in her. And since the divorce, she'd been too preoccupied with adjusting to single parenthood and launching the StrongGirls to even *think* about men.

But, really, a lack of time was just an excuse. She didn't have to deny herself male companionship forever. Ethan could be the one to draw her back into the land of dating and relationships. Still, it was never going to work if her potential boyfriend and her daughter couldn't be together in the same room.

ETHAN DECIDED to take Tony's advice to heart. He would do as much as he could to fix up the apartment, so Kat wouldn't be in a hurry to move out.

He waited until Kat and Sam left, and then he went to work. He hadn't asked Kat about entering her apartment, but he didn't think she'd mind since he was making legitimate improvements in his role as her landlord.

Tony was busy taking his test, but Ethan managed to recruit Priscilla to help. He opened the door and let her into the apartment ahead of him.

She gave a low whistle. "Man, this place is about as inviting as a prison cell."

No kidding. Kat still had only two pieces of furniture and a lamp in the main room. There were no pictures on the walls, no curtains, no books, no TV, no knickknacks. The bedroom was slightly more inviting, with colorful butterfly sheets on the bed and a pink beanbag chair in the corner. But the bed was resting on the floor; Samantha's toys were piled in a corner and her clothes were folded in cardboard boxes. She needed a toy box. Shelves. A dresser.

Then there were the dingy white walls, peeling trim and bare lightbulbs, which only looked worse now that the place had been so scantily furnished.

Kat had *said* she would get around to furnishing the apartment, but somehow, Ethan doubted she had the resources.

"We can get a lot done in a day," he said. "You know what my mom used to do? When someone new moved onto our block, she would organize a housewarming party. All the neighbors would get together, and they'd paint and fix things up. If the new people needed something like a crib or a high chair, someone always had an extra one."

Priscilla seemed fascinated. "That's cool. Something I never had growing up was a sense of community. We all drove into our attached garages and retreated to our yards behind our privacy fences. I knew a couple of neighbors, but that was it."

"You'll get community here. We have block parties, tree-planting parties, neighborhood yard sales."

"So let's do that for Kat and Samantha," Priscilla said, catching Ethan's enthusiasm. "We could call some of the guys from the station—they're always willing to lend a hand. Although…" She reconsidered. "You think they'd help us? They barely talk to us."

"We can try. It would be great if we could get it all done by the time Kat and Sam get home."

Ethan had hoped he could count on at least a couple of the guys to pitch in—for a struggling single mom and her kid, if not for him. But he was surprised by the response. By noon, he had four off-duty firefighters, two of their wives, the neighbor from across the street and his mother committed to the *While You Were Out*-style makeover.

"Oh, this is pitiful," his mother said, when she saw the barren apartment. "But, no matter. We can whip it into shape."

"That's why I called you, Mom. You're the general."

That she was. At four-foot-eleven and a hundred pounds, with short blond hair and bright pink lipstick, she still had more innate authority than anyone else. She divided the duties and assigned chores, and 250-pound firefighters were jumping to please her.

Tony joined them when he got home after taking his test. He brought a case of beer, just in case anyone needed incentive to see the project through. "Mrs. B!" He folded Ethan's mom in a bear hug.

"Careful, hon. You'll get paint on you."

"That's what I'm here for. Put me to work."

In addition to providing helping hands, the volunteers had brought furniture, paint, small appliances and a TV—all perfectly good stuff that wasn't being used. Ethan went to Lowe's and bought a new stove and fridge, which he'd intended to do anyway.

This little apartment was going to look ready for a magazine spread, by the time he was done. He couldn't wait to see Kat's reaction.

KAT'S FINAL MEETING of the day was a group counseling session with the Sunset High StrongGirls. She worked through the schools, which were only too happy to refer their "problem girls" to her and give her a place to meet.

This was her original StrongGirls group, and she would always have a special place in her heart for them.

The five girls and Kat met in the cafeteria, rather than in a classroom, so they could sit around a table informally. Kat usually bought them juice or milk from the vending machine and passed out granola bars. For some of them, it was the only healthy food they got all day. Yeah, it was charity, in a way. But they were still kids, and they couldn't learn and grow to be independent if they didn't have any fuel for their brains.

The girls greeted her excitedly. "Look, Ms. Kat, look what Tati has!" The speaker was Gwen, a tall, thin African-American girl with an amateur gang tattoo on her arm. She'd broken up with her drug-dealing boyfriend, at last, and was gradually pulling away from the gang herself.

Tati was Tatiana, a fifteen-year-old Hispanic girl with a shoplifting conviction. She'd come into the program with basement-level self-esteem, but gradually she was coming to realize she was pretty, smart and funny.

"What *does* Tati have?" Kat asked, trying to sound excited and expectant, rather than wary. The girls continually surprised her. Sometimes in a good way, sometimes not so good.

Today's surprise was a boy's class ring, heavily taped so it would fit on Tati's middle finger.

"Nice," Kat said as she passed out the granola bars.

"He wants to marry me," Tati said in a dreamy voice.

"He gonna *have* to marry you," said Stephie, an overweight girl who used her acerbic wit to protect herself from being hurt. "He gonna get you pregnant."

Kat cringed inwardly. Where did she begin cataloging the horrors of this situation? Tati was way too young to be talking about marriage. She was only a freshman, and the chances of her staying in school if she got married and started having babies were slim to none.

That was assuming that Romeo really did want to marry her, instead of just telling her that so she would sleep with him.

"Well, this provides a perfect entré into the subject I wanted to talk about today," Kat said briskly. "Sex."

Now she had their attention. She had ninety minutes in which to convince Tati she had more to offer the world than just warming some man's bed and birthing babies.

"Ms. Kat," Gwen said suddenly in a whisper. Her gaze darted toward the cafeteria door. "Who's that?"

Kat was surprised to see a tall good-looking silver-haired man standing in the doorway, watching silently.

"Oh, that's the same man that talked to me at the bus stop," said Stephie.

"Talked to you?"

"Yeah. He was asking me all about the StrongGirls."

"Really." Was he a parent with a problem teen? A reporter? A school official checking up on her?

She stood up, intending to talk to him and find out what the heck he was all about. But he disappeared, and when she looked outside there was no sign of him.

Just as a precaution, she warned the girls about talking to strangers, and they laughed at her. "You think I couldn't take down some scrawny, old white guy?" Gwen scoffed.

"Yeah, well, just the same. Y'all be careful."

By the time the session ended, she felt as if she'd made some progress with Tati in convincing her that having sex was *her* choice, not something she was obligated to do just to get a boyfriend or keep him. This was another heartfelt lesson Kat had learned the hard way.

"You have a boyfriend, Ms. Kat?" Tati asked.

"No, not right now." The image of Ethan floated into her imagination, along with memories of their bone-melting kiss.

"Then how do you know so much about sex?" Gwen asked.

That was a good question. Virginia had pointed out, more than once, that if Kat wanted to be a good relationship counselor, she needed to experience some relationships. One highly flawed marriage and some teenage backseat fumbling didn't cut it.

"I was once a teenager," Kat quipped. "I did a lot of things wrong and I learned from my mistakes, so you don't have to."

"Give us the gory details," Stephie said, leaning forward eagerly. "So we'll know exactly what not to do."

Kat laughed as she gathered up her materials. "I'll save that for another day." She hugged each of the girls in turn, a weekly ritual. Some had resisted at first, but now they all hugged back. If she did nothing else, she could at least do this.

As she drove to Samantha's after-school care, which was right across the street from her elementary school, she wondered if she *should* jump back into the dating pool—not just for the benefit of the StrongGirls, but for her own sake. She wasn't afraid of being without a man. But was there any reason to be alone when she didn't have to be? Pretending she didn't have time was a cop-out. She could manage to make time for things that were important. It was all a matter of priorities.

She thought of Ethan again. Then she remembered Samantha's feelings about their rescuer and her train of thought screeched to a halt. She still hadn't told Samantha that Ethan was their landlord, living just across the yard from them. She couldn't imagine what Sam would have to say if Kat announced she was *dating* Ethan.

Still, the thought produced a bubble of excitement that expanded inside her chest. What would it be like, having sex with Ethan? Then she chastised herself for even thinking of "sex" and "Ethan" in the same sentence. What had she just been preaching to the StrongGirls? A good relationship wasn't based on sex alone. It was based on mutual caring and respect. So far, Ethan had done all the caring, all the giving, and he hadn't let her do a thing.

She needed to change that, if there was any hope.

Chapter Six

By late afternoon, it was done. The walls were patched and painted a pale yellow; the kitchen had gleaming new appliances, attractive cabinets and counters, and a microwave, toaster and coffeepot; the twin bed now had a pale oak frame. There was also an oak table and four ladder-back chairs for the dining area, plus colorful throw rugs over the bare floors. One enterprising helper had even made curtains from donated sheets. The crisp white cotton billowed with the breeze that came in through the open windows.

"This looks fantastic," Ethan said as everyone hurried to clean up the painting tools and the last scraps of wood used to repair rotting window frames and baseboards. The results were better than he could have imagined. "I cannot thank all of you enough."

"We'll find a way to extract payment out of you," said Otis, as he headed out the door. He wasn't smiling, so Ethan wasn't sure if he was kidding or not. "I got some stumps that need taking out at my farm."

"Yeah, and you can mow my grass tomorrow," said

Jim Peterson. His wife punched him, but he didn't laugh. He just turned and departed. His wife gave Ethan an apologetic half smile and followed him. Soon everyone was gone except for Ethan, his mom and Tony.

"They're a strange bunch," Gloria Basque commented. "They seemed eager enough to work, but they were a little…reserved. Even the beer didn't loosen them up. Are these the men you work with?"

"'Fraid so," Tony said. "They're a tough crowd. Generous, but hard to impress."

"Yeah, well, the only ones I'm out to impress are Kat and Samantha," Ethan said.

His mother smiled. "Oh, I wish I could be here to see their faces. But I really need to go. It's my poker night."

"We should send Priscilla to play poker with you," Ethan muttered. "She'd get over that beginner's luck in a hurry."

His mom paused and looked around one more time at their decorating job. "It's really nice what you're doing for her, Ethan. She's a lucky lady."

"Hmph," Tony objected.

Ethan's hackles rose, but he waited until his mom was gone before he said anything. "What was that 'hmph' supposed to mean?"

"Just that I wouldn't call your motives entirely altruistic. I mean, you are hoping to get her into bed with all this," Tony said, gesturing to indicate the makeover. "Right?"

"No. I'm helping her out because she needs help. Period."

Tony crossed his arms. "And I suppose if she was old and fat and ugly, you'd still spend your entire paycheck on new appliances?"

Ethan opened his mouth, intending to voice a resounding *yes,* that the fact Kat was gorgeous and sexy had nothing to do with his altruistic activities. But he stopped.

Was he only being helpful because he wanted to be with her in bed? Was he using her bad luck as a way to ingratiate himself?

"You know it's true," Tony said. "Every girlfriend you've ever had was someone you had to rescue or fix."

"That's not…" But again, Ethan stopped. He thought back over the girls and women he'd dated—not all that many—and he couldn't think of a single one who'd been in a good place when he'd first been attracted to her. They'd all been in need of money or a job or a place to live or on crutches—or they'd been deeply depressed after being dumped by some other guy.

The downside was, after he helped them get back on track, they usually drifted off.

Did he have some kind of rescue complex?

Certainly, he'd helped out a lot of people who weren't potential girlfriends. Whenever his mom called him wanting some handyman work for a friend or neighbor in need, he jumped right in without question, and didn't expect anything in return except the satisfaction of doing a good job and a good deed.

Seeing that he'd hit home, Tony didn't belabor the point. He left, taking a load of trash with him.

Ethan was glad they'd all left. He wanted to have Kat's reaction to her much improved apartment all to himself.

Of course, he couldn't stay here to wait for her. As far as he knew, Samantha still didn't know who her landlord was, and he didn't want to surprise or upset the child with his unexpected presence.

SAMANTHA SEEMED TIRED after her first day back at school. She threw her backpack into the backseat, climbed into the front with a big sigh and buckled her seatbelt.

Where was the chattering magpie who jumped into the car every day full of stories about her day's adventures?

Kat gave her daughter a hug, then put the car into gear. "So, how was it?" she asked. "Did Mrs. Campbell help you with the work you missed on Friday?"

"Yeah, but I didn't miss much."

"That's good." At least Kat didn't have to worry about Samantha's academics. She'd learned to read when she was five and now she was at the top of her class. "What was the best thing that happened today?" This was a daily ritual they went through after school. Each of them had to tell the other about at least one positive experience.

"Nothing good happened."

Not an encouraging sign. "Did anything bad happen?"

Samantha sighed again. "Everyone was talking about the fire. They saw it on the news. They kept asking *me* to talk about it."

Oh, dear. "And did you?"

"No. I don't even remember what happened."

"You don't?"

"I don't want to remember," she amended. "Why can't they leave me alone?"

"They're just curious, honey. Most people have never been through a fire, and they want to know what it's like. But you don't have to talk about it—or even think about it—if you don't want to."

"I don't want to."

"Okay. All you have to do is say, 'I don't want to talk about it right now.'"

"That's what I did."

"Good girl. So *nothing* good happened?"

Samantha thought hard. "Mrs. Hanson, the cafeteria lady, put two cherries on my sundae."

"There you go! I knew you could do it. Want to know something good that happened to me?"

Samantha nodded.

"One of my StrongGirls got a job for the summer. It's her first-ever job. She's going to be a waitress so she can earn money for college."

Samantha relaxed into the conversation a bit, and Kat was looking forward to a calm, sane, boring evening for a change. But she wasn't going to get it. She realized that the moment she entered her new apartment.

"What in the world," she murmured. Had she walked into the wrong place? But no, there were the futon and the coffee table—and Bashira, meowing up a storm.

Otherwise, it sure didn't look like the same place. She set down her tote bag and took it all in.

She had a new kitchen. And a dining room table and chairs.

Samantha was equally dumbfounded. She walked through the main room and into the bedroom. "Mommy, I have a bed. A real bed."

Kat joined her daughter. The bed wasn't all. There was a small oak desk and a dresser, too. A toy box. Shelves. Curtains on the windows. Kat felt as if she'd dropped down a rabbit hole.

Samantha returned to the living room, craning her neck to look at everything. Finally, her gaze settled. "Look, Mommy, a TV!"

"Yes, that's what it is, all right."

"Can I turn it on?" She'd already found the remote and she was studying it.

"Uh… Sure, why not?" If the TV made this place feel like home for her daughter, then fine. She helped Samantha find a kid-friendly show. "Are you okay watching by yourself for a few minutes? I need to have a word with our landlord."

Samantha, already zoning out, nodded.

Kat locked the apartment door, went down the stairs, stomped across the yard, up onto Ethan's deck and to the back door. The lights were on inside and she could hear rock music. She banged on the door.

A few moments later Ethan opened the door looking good enough to eat, in soft faded jeans and a Brady's Tavern T-shirt. He smiled, which was enough to take the edge off her anger. Obviously, he thought he'd done something wonderful.

"Hi," he said, standing aside to let her into his kitchen. But when he read her expression, the smile disappeared. "Everything okay?"

"No, everything is not okay. What happened to my apartment while I was gone? I'd like to believe the furniture fairies paid me a visit, but somehow I doubt it!"

Ethan took in the furious bundle of female energy that had just invaded his kitchen and he could make no sense of it. She was angry?

Hell, how had he gotten this so wrong?

"I'm waiting for an explanation," Kat said, arms folded, foot tapping.

Ethan turned down the heat on some chicken he was frying. "We gave the place a makeover—me, Tony, Priscilla, some of the guys I work with. Even my mom. You…You don't like it?" Maybe yellow wasn't her favorite color.

"Whether I like it or not isn't the issue. You had no right." She clamped her mouth shut, then started again.

"Let me rephrase that. Yes, you own the property, and yes, you have a right to make improvements. But where did the furniture come from? And all those things in the kitchen?"

"The guys brought it over. It was just stuff people had."

"Castoffs." She made it sound like the most disgusting concept known to humankind.

"I know it's not Designer Showhouse stuff, but it'll do until you can buy what you want."

"I don't recall asking you to furnish my house."

"No, of course, you didn't ask. But you obviously needed some things."

"Yes. I did. But I was going to buy them myself."

"So now you can take your time. Kat, I don't understand why you're upset. There's nothing wrong with needing a little help now and then."

She clamped her eyes shut, then opened them again. "I don't *need* anything. I can take care of myself. And I certainly don't need charity."

"Is that what you call it? I call it one friend helping another."

"But we're not friends." He flinched, and she quickly backpedaled. "I mean, we weren't… We didn't even know each other until the fire, and every minute we've spent in each other's presence has had to do with you helping me, fixing my life."

"That's not how I see you."

"No? You just couldn't stand the thought of Samantha and me sitting on the floor to eat our meals, even though I was okay with it. Even though it was just going to be for a few days."

She was right about that. He couldn't stand thinking about her with no furniture.

"And the TV! I've been thinking how nice and quiet it was without one—how Samantha would spend more time reading and coloring and playing."

"Okay, I get the picture," Ethan said. "I thought you'd be pleased. But since you're obviously not, I'll take it all to the Salvation Army. Is that what you want?"

"Yes!"

She was the most frustrating woman he'd ever known. "That's just crazy!"

Kat opened her mouth and closed it again.

"I'm sorry," Ethan said softly. "I didn't mean that. But I really don't understand. Help me."

All the fire seemed to drain out of her. "You're right, it is a little crazy. And maybe if I explained some things, it would help. But right now, Samantha's expecting dinner, and I promised her some just-us-girls time. After she goes to bed—if I can get her to go to bed by herself— I'll come back. We'll talk." She slipped out the door.

"AND THEY LIVED happily ever after." Kat closed the Dr. Seuss book she'd been reading. It didn't really end with those words, but Samantha expected to hear them at the conclusion of every bedtime reading session, even if they had to stop in the middle of a book. She said she couldn't go to sleep if she was worried about the people in the story.

"Mommy, you get in bed with me."

"Sweetie, you're a big girl now. You've been sleeping in your own bed since you were a baby."

"But I can't go to sleep by myself." She chewed on one of her sparkly pink fingernails. They'd done each other's nails after dinner, and Sam had seemed more relaxed again.

"I bet you could if you tried." Kat set it up as a challenge. Samantha, every inch her mother's daughter, couldn't resist a challenge.

"Bet I couldn't."

"Tell you what. Let's give it fifteen minutes. I need to clean up the kitchen and get ready for tomorrow. I'll check back in fifteen minutes, and if you're not asleep I'll get in bed with you. Is that a deal?"

Samantha thought about it. "Okay."

"I love you, Sammy. And if you wake up or you're scared, you just call me and I'll be close by." She hugged Sam, kissed her, and hugged her again, then tucked her in and turned out the light.

In fifteen minutes, Samantha was fast asleep. Kat breathed a sigh of relief. She figured if she could get Samantha to sleep by herself for one night, she could break the pattern.

Now, for the other tricky task of the evening. She'd promised Ethan an explanation and she supposed he deserved one. She'd gone a little bit nonlinear on him, when he really thought he was helping. Her reaction had been a knee jerk and not very logical, and she could see that now. What harm was the loan of a few pieces of furniture that no one was using?

She tried to keep this in mind as she tiptoed out the door and down the stairs. Ethan was waiting for her on his deck. He lounged in one of the patio chairs, sipping a glass of red wine. The bottle and another glass sat on a glass-top table nearby.

He stood as she climbed the steps to the deck. "You got Samantha to bed okay?"

"Yeah. Kids who experience trauma, like a fire or a car accident, often revert to the behavior of a younger age. Samantha has never had problems at bedtime. She's slept in her own bed since she was an infant. So wanting me to stay with her is definitely unusual. But she went to sleep without tears tonight, so we're making progress."

"Good. It's only been a few days."

"I know." She chose another chair with a good view of her apartment and sank into it. The window to Samantha's bedroom was open a few inches, so Kat could hear if the child cried out, but she doubted that would happen. Sam, like her mother, was a hard sleeper.

Ethan filled the other wineglass and handed it to Kat. He hadn't asked if she wanted anything to drink, which rankled her slightly. But the fact was she did want a glass of wine. It was a beautiful spring evening, with the scent of honeysuckle heavy in the air. A couple of lightning bugs blinked crisscrossing patterns around the yard.

She didn't know how to ease into what she had to say, so she just started. "When you were younger, did you ever know one of those kids with mismatched socks and threadbare clothes, always a bit malnourished? Their hair looked like someone just hacked it off with a pair of dull scissors. They sat in the back of the classroom, never opening their mouth, hoping no one would notice them. Do you remember those kids?"

Ethan shrugged. "Sure. Every class has one, it seems."

"Well, I was one of those kids." She paused to let that sink in. "And did you ever have a toy drive at school, so the poor kids could have a toy under the tree? Or collect clothing for a poor family? Again, that was me.

"My mother never had a job in her life. She counted on men to take care of her. Sometimes they beat her up, and sometimes they beat *me* up—though I learned pretty quick how to stay under their radar."

She could see Ethan getting more and more agitated by her story, until he finally exploded. "Why didn't someone help you? Help her?"

"People did try. I got taken away from her twice. But she always cleaned up her act enough to get me back. I'm not sure why she bothered. I never saw the slightest indication she cared anything for me. Maybe she just wanted the welfare checks."

"What about your father?"

Kat shrugged with a nonchalance she didn't feel. These memories still had the power to make her cry, if she didn't guard herself. "Never knew him. Never even knew his name. There's no father listed on my birth certificate. Anyway, the church ladies used to show up at our apartment every few months with a garbage bag of clothes and some canned goods and macaroni. Every stick of furniture we owned was somebody else's castoff. I was seventeen, the first time I actually went into a store to buy new clothes."

"Oh, God. Kat."

"The last thing I want is for you to feel sorry for me. I'm only telling you this so you'll understand. Being forced to accept charity made me feel weak. Stupid. Not normal. And I swore, over and over, that when I was grown up I wouldn't ever, ever take anyone else's old stuff again. I would buy things new, or I wouldn't have them at all."

Of course, being married to Chuck, she'd accepted charity of an entirely different kind, but she hadn't seen it that way at the time. Chuck saw her at a bus stop on a rainy day and offered her a ride home, and she'd accepted. When he found out her situation—that her mother had just died, and no one was taking care of her—he'd taken her on as his special cause. He'd fed her, clothed her and found her a job. A year later, he'd married her. Then he'd put her through college, helping care for Samantha at night so she could attend classes or study. He'd wanted her to become a teacher.

But he hadn't really wanted her to become independent. She was his project, and he enjoyed being the savior and nurturer far more than he would ever admit.

When she got her master's degree and started working, pulling in her own salary and wanting a say in family decisions, Chuck had been devastated. He still expected her to be his teenage bride, looking up to him for everything.

They'd tried to make it work for another year, but there was no saving it. When they split, she made another vow. Not only would she always buy things new, she wouldn't depend on anyone for anything— because there was always a price. Chuck thought he could earn Kat's love by giving, giving, giving. But no matter how hard she tried, she couldn't love him, not the way a wife should love her husband. She was grateful, and at seventeen she hadn't known the difference between gratitude and love.

She still wasn't sure she could tell the difference.

Ethan drained his wineglass, not meeting her gaze.

"Did that help you understand?" she asked. "At all?"

"I think so. You…don't like secondhand stuff?" he ventured.

She sighed, exasperated. "No, Ethan. I don't like being seen as a charity case. I'm not the poor girl anymore. And when I saw that you and your buddies had donated all that stuff, everything I felt as a little girl came rushing back to me. That's what I want you to understand. I had a knee-jerk reaction, and I apologize for that."

"Do you really want me to move all the stuff out?"

"No." She had to laugh at herself. "Samantha likes her new bed, though she was quick to remind me it's not the canopy bed I promised. And it was nice to sit at a real table. So, no, ripping up the apartment and hauling everything to the Salvation Army isn't the answer. But I was wondering, could I pay for those things?"

She thought it was a perfectly reasonable request, a nice compromise, but Ethan looked pained. "I don't even remember who gave what. But even if I did, you might hurt people's feelings if you tried to pay them. Everybody felt good about pitching in. Why ruin that?"

She hadn't thought of it that way. She liked helping people, too. How many times had she provided the StrongGirls with something they needed? A secondhand computer to help with their schoolwork or a new outfit for a job interview? When any of her girls shunned her help, that hurt.

"Okay," she said. "And thank you. Please thank everyone again. In fact, I'll write thank-you notes, and you can deliver them."

"That's not..." He stopped. "Okay. Kat, where's your mother now?"

"She died when I was seventeen."

"I'm sorry."

She reached over and squeezed his hand, glad she'd made the effort to set everything straight. She didn't expect Ethan to hold her hand captive. He raised it to his lips and placed the softest of kisses on one knuckle, then the next, and the next. Kat's stomach quivered with the anticipation of each touch of his lips.

"I sh-should go." But she made no move to reclaim her hand.

Ethan ran one fingertip along her inner arm and she shivered. What was he doing to her?

"Are we okay, then?" he asked. "You're not angry anymore?"

She shook her head. Lord, no. She was feeling a lot of things—arousal, anticipation, some anxiety—but anger had fallen off the bottom of the list.

"So let's talk about us. Or maybe Samantha and me. Have you told her I'm living across the yard?"

"Not yet. I will tomorrow." If Sam happened to look out a window and see Ethan when she wasn't expecting to, it could freak her out.

"Let me know how it goes. If she's still afraid of me, we'll have to work on that. I'll do whatever it takes to earn her trust, Kat. Whatever it takes.

"Because I'm going to be seeing a lot of her mother."

Kat raised an eyebrow at him. He was still holding her hand, still tickling the inside of her arm.

"That's assuming her mother thinks that's a good idea. Does she?"

Kat resisted the urge to immediately say, yes, it was an excellent idea. "I haven't dated, at all, since my divorce two years ago," she told Ethan. "I'm not sure I even know how."

"It's real easy. I ask you to a movie. You say yes. We go, we have a good time, maybe get some coffee afterward."

Somehow, she didn't think it would be as simple as that. "I need to take things slowly, okay?" She knew she was overly cautious sometimes, but that was the best she could do.

Chapter Seven

"Mommy! Mommyyyyyy!"

Kat bolted upright, ripped abruptly from a deep sleep. She was at Samantha's bedside in an instant, relieved to find there was nothing obviously wrong. Sam was having a nightmare.

Her heart racing, Kat woke her daughter as gently as she could. "Sammy, honey, I'm right here. You're okay, you're safe. It's just a bad dream."

The little girl's eyes opened. "Fire? Is there a fire?"

"No, honey, there's no fire. It was just a dream. We're perfectly safe."

"Where's Bashira?" She looked around frantically.

"I'm sure he's around, somewhere. Bashira? Here, kitty, kitty." The cat was probably in the middle of Kat's futon, monopolizing the space. Since Samantha had shunned Bashira, the kitten had decided to sleep with Kat, and he liked to settle down right in the middle.

Bashira came trotting in to Sam's room, meowing, expecting a treat. He jumped up on the bed, and Samantha petted him.

"Dumb cat. I dreamed he got burned up."

"Oh, Samantha, that must have been scary. But here he is, safe and sound."

Bashira, craving attention, rubbed himself all over Sam. Eventually, she put her arms around him. Who could resist him, even with his ragged ears?

Kat sat on the edge of the bed and cuddled her daughter. "I hear sirens," Sam said. "I keep thinking they're coming here."

The sirens were loud. Kat hadn't thought about their proximity to station 59, when she'd moved in here. "That's just because we live so close to the fire station. They're not coming here. If there was any problem, our smoke alarms would go off. And I promise we'll hear them this time." The first purchase Kat had made was two heavy-duty extra-loud smoke detectors. She'd installed them herself and tested them. She'd let Samantha test them, too. The buzzers were loud enough to wake Kat, even if she was comatose. She'd also bought three fire extinguishers, one for each room. Maybe that was overkill, but the sight of all those red canisters was reassuring.

"If we had a fire, how do the firemen know where we are?" Samantha asked.

"That's a good question. And you know who would know the answer? Mr. Basque."

"Mr. Basque? Oh, the fireman." Sam's upturned nose wrinkled in distaste.

"Not just any fireman, but the one who rescued us. And Bashira. And I have to let you in on a little secret.

"This apartment…Mr. Basque owns it. He's letting us live here until we can find a bigger place. He's the one who fixed it up and painted the walls while we were gone today. In fact, he lives in the big house."

Samantha's eyes widened in alarm. "You mean that house right there? Right in the yard?" She pointed out the window. Although it was dark, she had the general direction right.

"Yes, that's the one."

"Is he there right now?"

"Yes. I imagine he's asleep."

"He won't come in here, will he?"

"Not unless we invite him. But Samantha, I think we should invite him. He's offered to go over every inch of this place and make sure we're one-hundred percent safe. He puts out fires every day, so he knows all about how fires start. Now who better to show *us* how to be safe?"

"I don't want him here."

"Even if it's just for a few minutes, so we can be safer? Personally, I'll sleep better at night knowing we've done everything we can to protect ourselves, and I bet you will, too."

Samantha wavered. "Will you be here?"

"Of course."

"Okay, I guess he can come over, but only for two minutes." Then she yawned. "Will you get in bed with me? Just until I fall back asleep."

Kat considered that a reasonable request.

They snuggled spoon fashion—Kat, Samantha and Bashira, who didn't seem to mind being squashed against Sam's stomach. He purred so loudly it sounded as if a small lawn mower was in bed with them.

At least Sam had regained her affection for her kitten. And she'd agreed to let Ethan come over, even if it was only for two minutes.

Baby steps.

ETHAN WHISTLED as he loaded sheets and towels from the B shift into a large-capacity washing machine. Laundry was an easy chore. He could do it whenever he decided to, so long as everything was dry and folded by the time his shift was over.

"Somebody's happy," said Priscilla, as Ethan wandered into the kitchen to find a snack. She and Tony sat at the table, playing poker.

"Are you guys still at it?"

"We've created a monster," Tony said. "Priscilla is the luckiest poker player I've ever seen, not to mention the most ruthless. She's bleeding me dry."

"Better quit while you're ahead," Ethan cautioned her. "Lucky streaks don't last forever."

"Not luck. Skill. I've got this game figured out. Any moron can win."

"We better check my IQ, then," Tony said, "'cause I'm losing my butt."

"You guys can't think of something better to do?"

"Like what?" Tony shuffled the cards and dealt another hand of five-card draw. "I suppose you've been engaged in some noble activity that gives you deep, inner satisfaction at the same time it's making the world a better place."

"No, I've been doing laundry," he admitted. He opened the C-shift fridge, frowned at the meager offerings, then checked the pantry. Half a box of chicken-flavored crackers. "We need to go shopping." He settled for a cold Diet Coke and sat down at the table. "Deal me in."

"So what's got you so chipper?" Tony asked. "Is it Kat?"

"Yeah, as a matter of fact. She asked me to come over tomorrow night." For a safety inspection, not a date, but still. If all went well, he planned to turn the evening into something more personal.

"Nice work," Tony said. "Think you'll get lucky?"

Priscilla kicked Tony under the table. "You're not in high school anymore. No wonder your girlfriends never stick around long, if you take that attitude."

"Hey, low blow."

"You're the one who told me your relationships have longevity issues. I didn't make it up."

Ethan was glad the conversation had turned away from Kat. She was too important to trivialize with talk of "getting lucky." She was special. And he had a date with her tomorrow.

Okay, it was only a two-minute date. But if he couldn't make progress with Samantha, there was still Plan B.

He'd wanted to kiss Kat again, when they'd been sitting on his deck drinking wine, but he'd settled for holding her hand. At least she wasn't mad at him. And she'd shared her painful past with him—something he didn't imagine she did too often. He felt honored that she'd trusted him with that information. And more determined than ever that she would never want for anything again.

IT WAS A WARM AFTERNOON when Ethan arrived at Kat's door for the fire safety inspection, and he was glad for the heat. Because when Kat opened the door she was wearing denim shorts, revealing her smooth, shapely legs, and a snug white T-shirt. He could see just the faint outline of her lacy bra through the clingy cotton, and it made his mouth grow dry.

She'd pulled her luxuriant hair into a thick braid that hung partway down her back, and she had on a bit of makeup. She might be dressed ultracasually, but she'd taken pains with her appearance.

That made his grin wider.

"What?"

"You just look so great, that's all." He stepped inside and looked around, pleased by what he saw. The place was starting to look like a home. Kat had added a few pictures on the walls, a vase of fresh flowers on the coffee table and a couple of throw pillows on the futon. "Where's Samantha?"

"In her room. Samantha!" she called. "Samantha. Come out, please. Mr. Basque is here."

Samantha appeared in the bedroom doorway, her expression wary. A Raggedy Ann doll dangled from one hand.

"Hi, Samantha," Ethan said, speaking softly and offering a reassuring smile.

It didn't work. She continued to stare at him with those huge eyes, so like her mother's.

"I brought something for you," Ethan said, digging into the plastic bag he'd carried in with him. "Captain Campeon has agreed to make you the official fire-safety marshal for 118 North Winnetka Street." He produced a child-sized red plastic firefighter's hat and a gold-colored tin badge. "Shall we pin the badge on your shirt?"

Samantha stepped forward a couple of feet. "I don't know how to be a safety marshal."

"That's why I'm here. I'm going to train you. When we're done, your apartment will be as safe as any place in Oak Cliff, maybe in all of Dallas."

She did not look convinced. Her gaze darted to her mother, then back at Ethan. She didn't move an inch from the doorway and looked ready to flee at the slightest provocation.

Kat went to Samantha and took her hand, which seemed to give the child a bit of courage. "Okay," Kat said. "Since I'm the assistant safety marshal, I'm ready to learn my stuff. Let's get started."

Ethan examined the outlets and light switches, which he already knew were perfectly safe since he'd checked them out before Kat and Sam moved in. He looked for frayed electrical cords. He examined all the fire extinguishers to see that they were fully charged, and then made sure both Kat and Samantha knew how to use them. He tested the smoke alarms and almost deafened himself.

"Where did you get those things?"

"The Safety Store," Kat said. "You can be sure I'll never sleep through a smoke alarm again."

Samantha dutifully followed Ethan around, watching and listening. He gave her a checklist and let her read it aloud, which she did amazingly well for a seven-year-old. When she finished, she looked up at Ethan quizzically.

"Do you really go to a fire every single day?"

"Well…not every day. When I first started this job, I went for two whole weeks without any fires, at all. Fires don't happen very often, you know. Most people go their whole lives without living through a fire like yours."

"But I hear sirens all the time, at night," Samantha said. Her voice grew fearful again. "What about all those fires? Don't they have safety marshals?"

"Most of those sirens you hear aren't fires. Sometimes it's the police, chasing down a speeder or something. Sometimes it is the fire truck you hear. But we get called out to all sorts of things—car wrecks, or when people get sick and need to go to the hospital. Even a funny smell. Usually, it's no big deal."

Her little face registered surprise. "Really?"

She'd ventured a little closer to him, though she still held Kat's hand in a death grip. He got down on one knee, so he could be at her level. "Really. Now, we've checked out your apartment, and it gets an A-plus-plus for safety. But do you know what to do if there is a fire?"

Kat took in a sharp breath. Samantha was doing really well so far. Ethan had been here at least ten minutes, and Sam hadn't tried to enforce the two-minute agreement. But this was straying dangerously close to the topic that got her all upset.

"I call 9-1-1," Samantha said solemnly.

"That's right. But you do it from the neighbor's house—after you get out. If you smell smoke or see flames, you don't stop to call anybody, you don't stop to grab anything."

"What about Bashira?"

"Cats are pretty smart about getting out of a fire. Bashira can take care of himself."

"Nuh-uh." Samantha shook her head fiercely. "Dumb cat was hiding under the bed."

Ethan looked at Kat, who shrugged. She couldn't see telling a child to leave her beloved pet behind in a fire, even if searching for Bashira was what had gotten them into trouble in the first place.

At least Sam was concerned about the cat's welfare. For a while, Kat had worried that Samantha blamed poor, hapless Bashira for the fact they almost hadn't escaped the fire.

"Mr. Basque, how does the fire truck know where to go?" Samantha asked.

"You give your address to the 9-1-1 operator, and she tells the driver of the fire truck. Then there's a computer right in the truck that shows a map of the whole city. It shows the driver exactly where to turn."

Samantha looked impressed.

Next, Ethan suggested they run through a fire drill. "You only have one door and no fire escape," he said, "and if your path to the door is blocked by smoke or fire, you need to learn how to go out the window."

Samantha, who'd been thawing out slightly, immediately tensed at the mention of fire, smoke and windows. "No. Mommy, I don't want to do the safety inspection—and it's been way more than two minutes." She clung to Kat.

Kat picked up her daughter and squeezed her reassuringly. "All right. I guess that's enough safety for one night. Do you want to pin on your badge and wear your hat?"

"No."

Kat looked at Ethan helplessly. "Can you thank Mr. Basque for helping us to be safe?"

"Thank you," she said, almost grudgingly, her face buried in her mother's shirt.

"I guess that's my cue to exit," Ethan said. The look he gave Kat spoke of regret and sadness. Kat knew his feelings were hurt, having a little girl reject him. Kat didn't feel too hot about it, either.

WHEN KAT SWUNG HOME for lunch the next day, she was feeling optimistic, despite her lack of sleep. A thunderstorm had blown in during the night, scaring Samantha silly. She'd never been afraid of storms before, but Kat had again found herself sharing the twin bed with her daughter and a cat.

That morning had dawned clear and pleasantly cool, however, the sky a brilliant blue. The air had a fresh-scrubbed after-storm scent to it. Everything looked green and shiny, and Sam had awakened cheerfully.

When Kat opened the gate, she was surprised to find Ethan in the backyard, using a circular saw to make a cut in a long four-by-four. He'd taken off his shirt, and for a few moments she paused to simply admire the play of muscles across his back as he worked.

When he set the saw down to make another measurement, she moved closer and he saw her.

"Hey, Kat." He smiled, his even, white teeth glinting in the sun.

"Hey, Ethan. What's all this?"

"It's a fire escape. Well, it will be. I was cleaning up some broken branches in the yard and I really looked at your windows, and I saw how high up they are. There's no safe place to jump."

"This is for my apartment?" she asked incredulously.

"It needs one. And I want you and Samantha to feel one-hundred percent safe. If she's scared at the idea of jumping out a window, now she won't have to be."

"But don't you think that's going a little overboard? We're not going to be living here that long."

His enthusiasm sagged a bit. "I'm improving the property, and a fire escape will benefit any tenant I end up with. Anyway, I enjoy this kind of thing. I'm not allowed to moonlight until I've been on the job a while, but I can at least work on my own projects."

Whether he enjoyed it wasn't the issue. Kat couldn't deny how uncomfortable this made her feel. Ethan was going to a lot of trouble for her. Paint and a new kitchen, he might have done anyway. But this? Lumber was expensive, and a fire escape was a huge project.

"I was going to buy us a rope ladder," she said.

"Now you don't have to. Is something wrong? I thought you'd be pleased. Is everything okay with Sam?"

"She had a bad night last night. The storm scared her." And maybe it was Kat's lack of sleep that had her overreacting today. "She seemed okay this morning. But I just don't know what to do with her sometimes, when she refuses to be comforted. I'm great at counseling other people's kids, but not my own." She wished she hadn't blurted out that last part. Ethan didn't need to hear about her maternal insecurities.

Bashira trotted up to greet her, and she leaned down to scratch him behind his ears. "How did you get outside?"

"I let him out," Ethan said. "He started howling at the open window when he saw me out here, and I felt sorry for him. And it's pretty hot today. I thought I'd go to Home Depot tonight and buy you an air conditioner. You won't survive long without one."

Of course she would survive. Did he think a little heat would shrivel her up? She'd been on her own for two years now and taking care of things just fine. The way Ethan just charged in, declaring she needed this and had to have that, unsettled her.

"It's very kind of you to go to so much trouble," she forced herself to say. "But you've already done so much. I mean, a brand-new kitchen, the cleaning, the paint… Anyway, we'll be out of your hair before it gets really hot."

"Kat, you're not in my hair. I couldn't sleep at night knowing you were living in an oven. I have to buy a window unit, anyway."

Virginia would counsel her to simply say thank-you. "Look, Ethan, just because you saved my life, that doesn't make you responsible for it for all eternity. You're worrying way too much about us."

He scratched his head. "Because I want to buy an air conditioner? To improve my rental property?"

She took a deep breath. Okay, maybe Virginia was right. "I'll shut up now. An air conditioner would be nice, so thank you. But don't feel like you have to rush out and buy it," she ended lamely.

"You're very welcome, Kat. I would do anything to make this time easier for you and Samantha."

How many times had Chuck said, *I would do anything…?*

"Thank you," she said again. "I have to grab some lunch—I've got a meeting with some school officials in a few minutes. I could make you a sandwich."

"You don't have to feed me," Ethan said.

She gave him a challenging look. "You're doing all this to help me out. And you won't accept one measly sandwich?"

"I already ate. Really. But thanks." He smiled again, and her insides went all gooey.

What was she to do with a man like Ethan? One side of her wanted to just tell him to back off. But the other side wanted to pull him closer, to feel those muscles on his back again—without a shirt.

She turned, and ran up to her apartment before she said or did something else that would make him think she was as confused as a squirrel in the middle of the street with a car bearing down.

Ethan returned to his carpentry, shaking his head. For all her college smarts, Kat Holiday was certifiable. Maybe he was going out of his way for her. He probably wouldn't have built an elaborate fire escape for just anyone. But he couldn't help it. She was going through a rough patch right now, and he wanted to help her. That was who he was and what he did. He couldn't stand to see anyone—man, woman, child or animal—suffering needlessly, especially not when it was in his power to fix things.

Wanting to help her out had nothing to do with the fact he'd been the one to drag her from a burning building. He would still want to help her, even if he'd not been involved in her fire.

But would he be so determined to help her if he wasn't attracted to her? If she didn't have those sultry brown eyes and that lush body?

Tony had asked Ethan that, and he'd vehemently denied that Kat's attractiveness had anything to do with his offering her his apartment and fixing it up so nice; that he would have done the same for anyone who'd come into his life in such dire straits. But was that really true?

He'd been unsure before, but he knew the answer now. No. He wanted to get closer to her, and he was doing anything and everything to remove the barriers—

including wooing her daughter. Unless Samantha accepted him, his chances with Kat were nil.

Unfortunately, his efforts weren't exactly producing the desired results. Kat's prickly reaction to the fire escape and the offer of an air conditioner left him bewildered.

Maybe it was time for Plan B.

Chapter Eight

"I think he sounds totally dreamy," Deb declared. Kat, Deb and Virginia were at the office sticking labels on donor-solicitation cards. "I'm not sure I understand your problem."

"I'm not sure I understand it, either," Kat confessed.

"Well, let's figure it out," said Virginia. The psychologist was in her fifties, dumpling soft, with short white hair and designer glasses. She had been Kat's thesis advisor at the University of North Texas and acted as her mentor when Kat began to put together StrongGirls. Kat had been thrilled when Virginia agreed to be on her staff, despite the fact Kat couldn't pay her anything near what she was worth. She'd needed someone with Virginia's impeccable credentials to give the program respectability, and she also valued Virginia's opinions and skills. The girls loved her, and Kat did, too.

Except when she wanted to analyze Kat, as she did now.

"Do you mistrust Ethan?" Virginia asked. "Do you think he has an ulterior motive?"

"Well, he's interested in me. Romantically."

"So he thinks doing all this stuff for you will further his cause?" Deb asked.

"I don't see how, when I've told him several times now to stop it."

"So really," Virginia said, "he's doing things for you, giving you things, out of the goodness of his heart. Because he thinks you need someone to take care of you—even at the risk of making you mad."

Virginia had nailed it. "That's it. He thinks I can't take care of myself. Which is one step away from making decisions for me."

"Like Chuck," Deb said. By now, Kat's two colleagues knew all about her ex-husband.

"Like Chuck," Kat agreed.

"Well, you *have* just been through a devastating fire," Virginia pointed out. She pushed her glasses down her nose and looked over them at Kat. "You lost everything, your child's health was affected and you were homeless. Let's face it, you would have appeared—at least to an outsider—pretty vulnerable."

"Oh, thanks, Virginia."

"She has a point," Deb said. "We know how strong you are, but he has to learn that about you. Give him a chance."

"I'm trying," Kat said. "But what if I get used to all this cosseting? What if I get spoiled, and start taking it for granted? That's what really scares me. Part of me *likes* being taken care of. Part of me wants to just relax and let him handle my problems for me."

"That's a perfectly natural feeling," Virginia said.

"Don't be so hard on yourself. And for heaven's sake, let him do things for you now and then, if it makes him feel like a hero. Don't sit so high on your pride that you drive him away before giving him a chance. Once he sees you're not going anywhere, he'll settle down."

Kat could only hope her friend was right, because she wanted a chance with Ethan. She really did.

ETHAN COULD HARDLY WAIT until Kat and Samantha got home that afternoon. He had a surprise for Samantha that was sure to bring a smile to her face. It pierced him to his heart every time she looked at him with those wary eyes.

When he heard Kat's car he went out onto the deck, ready to intercept them as they came through the gate.

"And then Mrs. Campbell got really mad," Samantha was saying as they entered the yard, "and Brittany had to go for a time-out!"

"Well, Brittany should have known bet—" She stopped when she spotted Ethan, standing on the deck.

Samantha instinctively grabbed her mother's hand, as if afraid Ethan was going to reach out and snatch her away. "Hi, Mr. Basque," she said cautiously.

"Samantha, I have a surprise for you."

"For me? What is it?"

Now Kat was the one who looked wary. "Ethan, haven't we talked about this—"

"It's not like that," he said quickly, taking the few steps from his deck down into the yard. He had the surprise behind his back. "This isn't something you need. It's purely for fun."

Just then, his surprise made a yipping sound.

Samantha's eyes got huge. "Is that a puppy?" She looked up at her mother, delighted.

Ethan brought the squirming spotted pup from behind his back.

"It's a puppy!" Samantha squealed, as she opened both arms. This was more the reaction he'd hoped to see the first time he showed Daisy's pups to Samantha. "Mommy, look, a Dalmatian! Can I name him Pongo?"

Ethan laughed. "Well, considering it's a girl, I'm not sure that's appropriate."

Samantha set the puppy down on the grass and got down on her hands and knees. "C'mere, puppy. C'mere!" She slapped her leg and the puppy toddled over, eager to play.

Ethan grinned broadly as he watched Sam interact with her new friend. Until he looked over at Kat and realized she was not pleased. Furious was more like it.

She grabbed him by the arm and dragged him several feet away, nearly toppling him. "*Why* on *earth* would you give my daughter a puppy without asking me first?"

"You don't think she should have a puppy?"

"No! We already have one pet. How could you think—"

"But look at her. She's having a blast."

He had her there. But not for long. "Ethan. Dogs are expensive. That is a purebred Dalmatian. How much did she cost?"

"Not so much." Three hundred dollars—which he had gladly paid to John Simon's widow, who was technically Daisy's owner. He couldn't *not* adopt one, not when Captain Campeon was threatening to take the whole lot to the pound if they didn't find homes soon.

"Dogs are time-consuming. They're smelly. They're destructive. And that thing is going to get *huge*."

"I'll pay for her food and vet bills and whatnot."

She pinched the bridge of her nose. "Somehow, I knew you'd say that. Yet one more thing I would owe you."

"Kat, this is something I wanted to do. You don't owe me anything."

"Just undying gratitude," she murmured.

"Not even that. Seeing Samantha laugh is payment enough. And maybe she'll stop looking at me like I'm toxic waste."

"You're trying to buy her affection," Kat said, and her voice rose.

Ethan shrugged uncomfortably. "If that's what it takes, yeah."

"We can't keep the puppy, Ethan. When we move, we won't be able to take her with us. You can't keep a dog that big in an apartment. And I'm not the one who's going to tell Sam. That's your problem."

Ethan started to throw out another argument, but then he heard a noise that stopped him. Kat heard it, too—a wheezing, whistling noise. They both looked toward the source of it.

Samantha was bent over at the waist and was clawing at her chest, obviously in the throes of a very sudden and very violent asthma attack.

Kat was at her daughter's side instantly, digging into

the child's backpack. "Take it easy, sweetheart. Where's your inhaler?"

Samantha shook her head. "Don't…know."

Kat jumped up. "I've got another inside. I'll be right back." She gave Ethan a pleading look before she jogged toward the garage and up the stairs.

Ethan dropped to his knees beside Samantha. Oh, God, he hoped it wasn't the dog that had triggered her asthma. It had never occurred to him that she might be allergic. "Breathe slow and easy, Sam," he said in his most soothing voice. "You're gonna be fine. Your mom's gone to find your inhaler."

Ethan had barely started his paramedic training, but he recognized that this was a pretty severe attack. Samantha's face was wet with tears; she was fighting for every breath and her face was red. "Don't fight your breath. Breathe slow and deep. You're gonna be fine."

He lightly rubbed her back, hoping to comfort her.

"Were you and Mommy…fighting?" Samantha asked. Every labored breath was like a slap in the face to Ethan.

"Oh, that," he said, as if it were no big deal. "We were just letting off some steam. We didn't mean anything by it. Sometimes people get into arguments about dumb stuff. But we should never have even started bickering."

She coughed a few more times, then gradually straightened up. Although her breathing was still labored, Ethan thought she sounded slightly better.

Samantha sank down to the grass, as if she were exhausted. "Why was Mommy mad?"

Ethan debated, then decided the truth was his best option. "I gave you a puppy without asking her first. Big mistake." He settled down beside her and continued to rub her back.

The puppy, completely oblivious to the drama, had rolled onto its back, and Ethan patted her tummy with his free hand.

"You were *giving* it…to me?" Samantha asked, incredulous.

"It's more like a loan," he hedged. "But you can play with her whenever you want. And you can name her, how 'bout that?"

She managed a smile and a nod. "Okay."

She was definitely breathing easier now, and by the time Kat returned with the spare inhaler the situation wasn't quite so scary. Samantha took a couple of hits and sounded better still.

"Mommy, don't be mad at Mr. Basque. He didn't really give me the puppy but he said I can play with her—" she paused to breathe "—whenever I want. And name her."

"We'll talk about the puppy later."

"Is she allergic to dogs?" Ethan asked.

"Not that I know of."

"I should have asked you that before. I'm sorry. This time you were right."

"And I wasn't the other times?" But she offered him a faint smile. Then she turned her attention back to her daughter. "Are you okay, now, Sammy?" Kat asked, smoothing a stray curl off the child's face.

Samantha nodded. "I ran too much, I think."

"That's okay, sweetie, it's not your fault. Do you think you left your inhaler at school?"

She nodded.

"Let's go inside and cool off."

"Can I show the puppy to Jasmine?" She and Jasmine had played together one afternoon already, and they seemed to get along very well.

"Maybe you can show Jasmine tomorrow." Kat helped Sam to her feet and took her hand. "And you," she said to Ethan. "We'll talk later."

KAT'S HEART was in her throat. She'd heard a little of what Ethan had said to Sam. He had known exactly what to do, what to say to calm her down, and now Kat felt like a heel. Ethan had only wanted to make her daughter smile, and she'd practically spit in his face.

On top of that, she'd lost her temper, upset Samantha and set a terrible example.

But she wasn't going to beat herself up over this. She was going to learn from it and move forward.

She ran a lukewarm bath for her daughter and fixed them some dinner. Sam played quietly with Bashira, then willingly got into bed and listened with sleepy eyes as Kat read from *Winnie the Pooh*.

"Mommy?" Samantha said suddenly. "Can I name the puppy Winnie?"

"You'll have to ask Mr. Basque."

"He said I could name her anything I wanted."

"Well, then, I think Winnie is a fine name."

"Do you like Mr. Basque?"

"Yes, I like him very much."

"I think I'm starting to like him, too. He's not scary like before."

"I'm glad, Sammy. 'Cause I think he's a really good man. He has a big heart." Kat gave her daughter a kiss and smoothed her hair off her face. She was so precious. Kat was once again overwhelmed by how lucky she was—how lucky they both were—to be alive.

Samantha closed her eyes, and Kat turned out the light and tiptoed out. She looked out the window and saw that Ethan was on his deck.

Waiting for her.

She brushed her hair, slipped on a pair of flip-flops and went downstairs and across the yard.

This time he was on the porch swing, and he patted the spot next to him. The puppy was at Ethan's feet, gnawing on his shoelaces.

"Well, let me have a look at her," Kat said, picking up the puppy before taking her spot on the swing. She held the spotted dog and looked her in the eye. "You are going to be a lot of trouble, Winnie."

"Winnie?"

"That's what Sam wants to name her."

Ethan shrugged. "It's a good enough name."

The puppy tried to lick her nose, and Kat set her back down. Winnie then found a rawhide chew and settled in to sharpen her teeth.

"I'm not very good at this relationship stuff," Kat said. "When I was married, Chuck and I had our assigned roles. He made decisions, and I followed them. At some point, I realized that wasn't right. I wanted to be on an equal footing with him. And he didn't like that, so we parted."

Ethan pushed the swing gently. "I'm certainly no expert, either. As I've clearly demonstrated."

Kat laughed. "It's hard. All the negotiating, the compromising. For a while, now, I've thought that being independent and standing strong were the most important things any woman could do. But if that means always getting your own way... Well, now I'm not so sure."

"No one gets it right on the first try," he said.

They lapsed into silence. The porch swing squeaked rhythmically and Kat decided it was one of the nicer moments of her life—simply because it felt so ordinary.

"Samantha has decided she likes you," she said.

"So bribing her worked?"

"Showing her you really care is what worked. Talking to her like she was a real person. Being gentle. That's what won her over. Not a puppy."

"I like her, too," Ethan said softly. "She's a great kid." He slid across the porch swing and put his arm around Kat's shoulders, drawing her close.

Kat was the one who felt a little bit crazy. At least, all sorts of wild thoughts were assailing her as she breathed in the masculine scents that clung to him. The good, clean smell of soap and the remnants of his citrus aftershave and... Spices. Rosemary, garlic, marjoram. He'd been cooking. She'd never known a guy who cooked, other than the occasional steak or burger.

"I could split the cost of the puppy's..."

"Don't even think about it."

She sighed. "I'm doing it again."

"So am I. We're a pair, huh?" He stroked her hair, seeming perfectly content to sit there, enjoying the evening breeze, listening to the chimney swifts as they darted and swooped overhead.

After several minutes, with a gentle hand on her chin, Ethan tipped her face up toward his, and she knew he was going to kiss her—and she knew she was going to let him. She felt more connected to Ethan at this moment than she had to any other man, ever. A warm glow descended on her, on them, and she eagerly met his mouth with hers.

His kiss was both gentle and demanding, his tongue a bold but welcome invader. He buried his hands in her hair, angling her head to give him better access. The kiss was so powerful that they lost their balance and nearly fell out of the swing. Ethan shot one leg out to steady them. His hand wandered to her breast, caressing her lightly through her shirt.

Heat blasted through Kat's body as she clutched the sleeve of his T-shirt. How she wanted to feel his bare skin. She could imagine clothes flying, his hands all over her naked body.

Unfortunately, they were on Ethan's deck, where any of their neighbors might see them. Not to mention Samantha.

"We have to stop," Kat gasped, breathing in great gulps of air.

"I know," he said on a groan.

"We need to take this slow, anyway," she said apologetically.

"I know that, too. I don't want to make any more false moves."

"When Samantha goes to stay with her father, maybe we can go on a date—a real date." But if Samantha wasn't around, would anything prevent Kat from letting her passions run wild?

ETHAN'S HOUSE was dark and quiet, now that the puppy had finally gone to sleep in her crate with the aid of an old alarm clock and a hot water bottle. But Ethan was too wound up to sleep.

He still couldn't believe how well things had ended up today, given how badly they'd gone earlier.

He'd learned an important lesson. Kat really, really didn't like him to make decisions for her. She wasn't just protesting about the gifts because she was polite or because she didn't believe she deserved them.

He actually offended her by giving her things she could acquire for herself and diminished her by giving her things she couldn't otherwise have—like a dog for her child. He made her feel as if he thought she was weak and incompetent to manage her life.

He was only coming to realize just exactly how strong—and strong-willed—she was. He had to learn to respect Kat's castle walls. He'd never met a woman so determined to stand alone, to take care of herself and her child with no help or interference. But that was her right, and he had to respect it.

He considered it a minor miracle that she was willing to let him get this close, this fast. And a real gift that Samantha was coming to accept him in her life, too. But he was going to blow it if he didn't back off trying to "fix" her life, a life she obviously believed did not need fixing.

Strange how things happened for a reason. He would never in a million years have wished illness on a child, but at least Samantha's asthma attack had defused his and Kat's tempers and forced them to see how unreasonable their behavior was.

Ethan managed to catch a few hours' sleep before his shift. He showered, shaved and changed into his uniform, then tucked the pup under his arm and walked the two blocks to the station.

He arrived early, hoping to slip Winnie back into the dog run with Daisy before anyone saw him. The pup couldn't stay by herself for twenty-four hours until she was older, and he didn't think asking Kat to care for her would go over well.

That would come in time.

Jim Peterson had brought a dozen tomato plants to put in the garden out back and after breakfast, when Captain Campeon was handing out tasks for the day, Ethan offered to transplant them.

"Then who's going to scrub the toilets?" the captain asked with a straight face, before he actually smiled. "Nah, go ahead."

"I was gonna do the garden," Peterson objected. "No one's touched it since Dave Latier…"

Ethan hadn't realized he would be stepping on anyone's toes or disrespecting one of the fallen firefighters. But that was exactly what Jim Peterson thought. A couple of the others agreed, if the resentful glances shooting his way meant anything.

"I'm sure there's no shortage of gardening to be done," the captain said mildly, refusing to involve himself.

Ethan would have gladly given the garden task to Peterson, if it would keep the peace, but the other man stomped out of the dining hall.

Well, hell. Ethan was stuck with the chore now.

Actually, he loved digging in the dirt. He loved the scent of freshly mown grass and the satisfaction of growing fat beefsteak tomatoes and bell peppers. As he worked to clear debris from last year's garden, he shook off his irritation. When it came to fitting in here at Station 59, sometimes it seemed he took one step forward and two steps back. Still, he was making progress.

Priscilla joined him a few minutes later, and they worked in companionable silence pulling weeds.

"I didn't know David Latier," Priscilla said, "but I'm sure the man wouldn't begrudge a couple of rookies working on his garden."

Ethan agreed.

"So, did you give Samantha her puppy?" Priscilla asked.

Ethan smiled. "Sam and I are going to share her."

"Look at you. You're grinning like a chimpanzee. You look just like Tony did when he first met what's-her-name from the academy. Must be true luuuuuuv."

Priscilla took a dead vine from the garden and looped it around Ethan's neck, then draped it over his head.

He snatched the vine away, laughing. "Don't even think of comparing me to Tony. I don't fall in love once a month like him."

"True. But now that you're in love, you've got that same sappy grin and that oh-ain't-it-good-to-be-alive attitude. Sorta makes me sick."

"I'm not in love," Ethan said quickly. He busied himself digging a hole for the next tomato plant. "I don't even know Kat that well."

"Doesn't matter. Face it, you're in love. I recognize the signs."

"How would you know? Have you ever been in love, Ice Princess?"

"No, I haven't, and don't call me that."

"So why don't you date? You're pretty, intelligent, well-educated. Any guy would go out with you."

"Do you see any guys hitting on me?"

"Well, no." Except for the drunk at Brady's. Which was a tad odd. Priscilla wasn't just pretty, she was a knockout. But she did give off definite keep-away-from-me vibes. Even Tony, who flirted with every woman he came into contact with, from the grocery-store checker to the eighty-year-old woman who walked her Chihuahua down their street every day, had learned not to flirt with Priscilla.

Ethan wisely decided not to point out that her Ice Princess nickname wasn't entirely undeserved.

"Don't you, like, want to hook up with anybody?" Ethan asked gingerly.

"I get all the male companionship I could possibly need. I live at a firehouse with nothing but men. I have one living downstairs from me and another next door. Why would I want to date one?"

"Oh, I dunno." He paused strategically. "Oh, here's an idea. For sex?"

She punched him on the arm.

"Ow. Cut it out."

"Women aren't like guys. We don't need sex the way we need air, like men think they do. It's nice when we can get it, but it's not that high on my priority list. Frankly, given all the crap you have to put up with just to have sex, sometimes it's not worth it."

Ethan thought about Kat and the steamy kiss they'd shared last night, and he couldn't help grinning again. She was definitely going to be worth it. "Then you're not doing it right."

Chapter Nine

"*How* much is it going to cost?" Kat asked her regular mechanic, thinking she hadn't heard right.

"Twelve hundred, give or take," said the mechanic, repeating what he'd already told her once, disregarding the note of panic in her voice. "You got a cracked head gasket, and your cam and crank sensors have been damaged, too."

She had not a clue what all that meant.

She'd started out that morning feeling pretty optimistic about how the week had gone. The company that handled her renters' insurance had finally come through with a check. She'd thought, since she'd lost *everything,* she would get the full amount of her policy. But no, there were loopholes. Still, the check was enough to let her pay off a good chunk of her credit-card balance and sock away a few hundred for emergencies.

Samantha was doing better. Her teacher reported that she was back to her usual self. She'd been helping Ethan take care of Winnie, and the two of them had walked the pup down the block and back. Jasmine had taken Sam under her wing, too, and the two girls had played together several times.

Kat had new StrongGirls groups forming for the summer, and she'd hired two wonderful new counselors. *The Dallas Morning News* had run a small article on Kat, and as a result she had several schools calling to get more information.

And then there was Ethan. He'd been terrific, seemingly happy to spend time with Kat, though her daughter had constantly been their chaperone. He'd bought and installed a large window-unit air conditioner, which she hadn't yet turned on because they'd been treated to a rare May cool spell. But other than that, he'd not tried to give her anything, help her with anything or in any way tried to tell her how to live her life.

She'd been on her way to an appointment with a school principal at Woodrow Wilson High that afternoon, singing to the radio. Then her car had started to make the most god-awful racket, clattering and smoking. She managed to get it off the freeway and coast to a stop on the service road, before she'd called the auto club.

Twelve hundred dollars. Could that be right? But she had no reason to doubt the mechanic, known as Mr. Bill, who'd been taking care of her little car for two years. He knew it inside and out and he was honest, if not terribly fast.

"You oughtta just get a new car," Mr. Bill said. "I

could sell you that sweet little Mustang over there for forty-five hundred."

"Mr. Bill, if I had forty-five hundred, I wouldn't be sweating the twelve hundred for the repairs! But never mind. Just fix my car—I'll have the money for you." Even if she had to run up her credit card. Again.

He required a down payment, so she drained her checking account.

What the heck was she supposed to do for groceries? A couple of days ago she'd deposited her insurance settlement check *and* her paycheck, but they wouldn't clear until Monday at the earliest.

Mr. Bill loaned her a clunker—an ancient station wagon in a peculiar shade of green—to use until her car was fixed. She had to doubt her mechanic's abilities as she drove away from the garage. Her loaner sounded as if it might have hamsters in the engine, running on little wheels.

She'd rescheduled her afternoon appointment, but still she was almost late picking up Samantha from after-school care.

"Whose car is this?" Sam asked as she climbed in and fussed with the seat belt.

"Ours is in the shop. This is a loaner." She didn't want to dwell on that, however. "So how was your last day of school?" Kat asked, forcing some enthusiasm into her voice.

"It was good. We had a party with cupcakes, and I'm officially a second-grader. We played Red Rover and I didn't have to use my inhaler even once."

The good news cheered Kat considerably. "That's great, Sammy. Maybe you're outgrowing your asthma. Wouldn't that be nice?" Kat could only hope. "I'm very proud of you for graduating from first grade."

"Me, too. So that's my good thing. What's yours?"

Oh, shoot. Kat usually had an answer ready, but today she was unprepared. "Mmm, let me think about it for a minute. Oh, okay, I know. I made every light on Jefferson."

Samantha laughed. "You can't do better than that?"

"Okay. I'll try harder." She thought a minute. "I know. I have a new StrongGirls group forming at Woodrow Wilson High."

"You used that one yesterday."

"I did?" She thought some more. Surely something good happened. She'd been in a good mood before her car had broken down. "Oh, oh, I really have it this time. I got a phone call from the mother of one of the StrongGirls. She wanted to thank me because for the first time in three years, her daughter had passed all her classes and doesn't have to go to summer school."

"That's real good," Samantha said. "Mommy, I'm proud of you."

"Me, too." She reached over and squeezed Samantha's hand.

"So, what are we having for dinner tonight?"

Yikes. A trip to the grocery store was out of the question until Monday. She had some odds and ends, and they could get by, but she'd been planning to fix a nice meal.

Sam cocked her head quizzically. "Does this mean we can have frozen waffles again for dinner?"

Oh, Lord. She couldn't do that to her growing daughter, not again. She could put her groceries on VISA, but she hated to do that.

"How about Everything Stew?" she suggested.

Sam wrinkled her nose. "It turned out kinda weird last time we made that."

"But that's the fun of Everything Stew. It turns out different every time." She'd learned about Everything Stew from one of the foster families she'd stayed with briefly. When you had people to feed and not enough of any one thing to make a meal, you put it all together in one pot. As long as she had some canned broth to start with—and she did—it usually turned out pretty good. Except for the most recent batch. The eggplant had been a mistake.

"Okay," Samantha agreed. "Can we put waffles in it this time?"

Hmm, waffle dumplings. Might not be as bad as it sounded.

Samantha giggled. "Ick, Mommy, I'm just kidding."

"Oh." Phew. She was glad to see Samantha recovering her sense of humor.

When they pulled into the driveway, they found Ethan trimming bushes in the front yard. Winnie was tethered to the porch railing. As little as she was, she still had a tendency to wander off.

Samantha barreled out of the station wagon and ran toward Ethan, then skidded to a halt just before ramming into him. They weren't yet at the hugging stage. Sam had never been quick to trust new people and she wasn't a natural hugger. But Kat hadn't started out in life a hugger, either. Instead, Samantha dropped down to pet Winnie.

"Ethan, guess what?"

It hadn't escaped Kat's attention that her daughter had started referring to Ethan by his first name, instead of Mr. Basque. She supposed that was okay. He'd probably told her to do it.

"Hey, Sam!" he greeted her. "Wait, let me guess. Today's your last day of school?"

"Well, yeah, but that's not what I was gonna say."

"Then what?"

"Mom and me are making Everything Stew."

"Everything Stew? I never heard of that."

"It's easy. You just throw in a little of whatever you can find. Except not eggplant. And not waffles."

Kat was getting more embarrassed by the minute. She'd just as soon Ethan didn't know about her pathetic excuse for dinner plans.

Ethan put down his tools, straightened, and walked up to Kat, who had opened the back door of her clunker to retrieve her briefcase and purse.

"Where'd this car come from?"

"Oh, well, I had a little car trouble today. This is a loaner."

"Why didn't you call me? I was home, I could have come to get you. And you could borrow my car. I'm sure it's safer than this thing."

"Hey, don't insult my wheels," she said, trying to keep the mood light. "It's safe. My mechanic is a good guy. He wouldn't loan me a car that wasn't safe."

"Does it have airbags?"

"No, but my car doesn't have them, either. That's why we wear seat belts." She waited, wondering if he would challenge her further, insist she do better. But he didn't. He must have been biting his lip, but he didn't pursue the argument, and she wanted to hug him for it. Chuck, bless his heart, would never have shown such restraint.

Maybe there was hope yet.

"C'mon, Sam," she said, "let's go see Bashira and get our dinner started."

"Are you really going to fix Everything Stew?" Ethan asked.

"We are," Kat said emphatically. "Would you like to join us?" *Please say no.*

"Actually, the guys next door are having a cookout. Jasmine is here, and she's staying the next two weeks. They're celebrating school letting out."

"Oh. Well, have fun. It sounds like a good time."

He pinched the bridge of his nose. "I wasn't telling you so you could send me off with your good wishes. You're invited, too."

"Can we, Mommy?"

Kat had to admit, the prospect sounded better than Everything Stew. Her mouth watered at the thought of grilled hamburgers. But she wondered whether Tony had really invited them, or if Ethan just assumed they would be welcome.

"All right, that would be really nice."

"Things'll get started about six. We can walk over together."

WHEN THEY ARRIVED at Tony's and Priscilla's house a little after six, Jasmine answered the door. "The party's out back on the deck," she said brightly. "Hey, Samantha, want to see my new Barbie?"

Sam nodded in mute adoration, and the two girls rushed off to Jasmine's room.

"I'm glad they're getting along so well," Ethan said.

"Me, too. In our old building, there weren't any children even close to Sam's age."

They wandered through the apartment, to the kitchen and out the back door to a gorgeous two-level deck, where a partylike atmosphere prevailed. The Gypsy Kings blared from a boom box. Tony presided over the grill, where hamburgers and hot dogs sent out mouth-watering smells. Priscilla was there, too, lounging in a hammock with a beer. Another couple whom Kat had never met were laying out the buns and condiments on a picnic table. Ethan, who'd brought Winnie with him, turned her loose in the backyard to play with another little spotted dog, undoubtedly one of her litter mates.

Kat felt a little bit like a gate-crasher, until Tony put down his spatula to give her a bear hug. "I'm glad you could come."

"Thanks for including us. I brought brownies." She hadn't wanted to show up empty-handed, so she'd thrown together a batch of brownies from a box. They'd gone over pretty well the last time she'd served them, at the fire station.

Ethan introduced her to the other couple, who were Jasmine's mother, Natalie, and her stepfather, Paolo. Kat thought it a bit strange that Tony socialized with his ex and her husband. Kat and Chuck got along pretty well—better than most divorced couples—but she would have found it awkward to attend a dinner at his house. She found the lack of tension refreshing.

A few minutes later, Ethan's mom arrived with a macaroni salad and a big smile for Kat. "Are you getting settled into your new place okay?" she asked. "Do you need anything?"

"We're doing well and I can't think of a thing we need, but thanks for asking."

Gloria elbowed Ethan. "She's so polite. Did you know she sent me a thank-you note?"

Tony laughed. "She sent me one, too."

"Me, too," said Priscilla.

"Well, it was just so nice," Gloria said. "Your mama must have raised you right."

Oh, if she only knew. Chuck's mother was the one who'd taught her how to write a thank-you note. Her mother-in-law had been very kind to the socially awkward waif her son had married.

Despite the party atmosphere, Kat was subdued during dinner. Maybe it was just the end of a long week. But she kept thinking about the Everything Stew and what Ethan must think of her, resorting to feeding her daughter something that sounded so unappealing.

The stew really turned out pretty good most of the time, and it was one way to get Sam to eat her vegetables. But Ethan didn't know that. Once again, Kat had given Ethan the impression she couldn't take care of herself.

And maybe she couldn't. Right now her budget was stretched to the limit, and the unanticipated car repair was a blow. Chuck had offered to take Samantha for the summer, to save Kat the cost of daycare. Brenda was home with the new baby, anyway. But Kat had declined the offer. Brenda had enough stress with a baby, and Sam was just now getting used to her new living arrangements.

Was that the right decision? Chuck wasn't wealthy, but he earned a decent amount as a pharmaceutical sales rep. She'd be willing to bet Chuck and Brenda never ate Everything Stew.

"You're quiet tonight," Ethan commented after dinner. The others had gathered in the den to watch a new reality show, but Ethan and Kat remained outside in the hammock, enjoying the breeze. Summer was around the corner, and soon cool evenings would be but a memory.

"I'm okay," Kat said, not wanting Ethan to worry. "This yard is really nice." Tall pecan trees gave the space an air of seclusion, providing a thick green canopy that was highlighted with a few landscape lights. The lawn was thick and lush, with a winding stone path and a birdbath at the end of it.

"Tony's been working on it. You know, before, he always lived in big, generic apartment complexes and he never cared about grass or trees. But the second he moved in here, he went crazy. It was a jungle back here when he started a few weeks ago."

"How long have you guys known each other?"

Ethan smiled fondly. "Since we were ten. I jumped in to 'save' him when he was getting beat up by a gang of big kids, and I ended up getting beat up myself. We've been best friends ever since."

Somehow, the story didn't surprise Kat. Ethan had probably been rescuing people since he could walk.

"So what happened to your car?" he asked. "You weren't in an accident, were you?"

"No. It's an engine problem."

"You could have let me take a look at it. Between us, Tony and I are pretty good with cars."

"Can you fix a cracked head gasket?"

"Oh." He let that sink in. "That's bad. It's gonna cost a fortune. Why don't you let me—"

"No, Ethan, I can manage. I'm not destitute."

"You can't buy groceries. How're you gonna pay for a cracked head gasket?"

"I have money," she said, a bit hotly. "I deposited two checks this week, but they haven't cleared yet—that's all."

"How are you going to eat the rest of the weekend? And please don't say Everything Stew. It bothers me, just thinking about it."

If she were honest, it bothered her, too. She'd been so relieved to have a hamburger instead. But what about tomorrow? She had tuna fish, but no mayonnaise. Macaroni, but no cheese. Peanut butter, but no jelly.

Her face grew hot and her eyes smarted. She was a StrongGirl. This was a short-term problem, and everything would be fine on Monday. But the tears came, anyway.

"Oh, Kat." Ethan enfolded her in his arms. "You don't have to cry. You can come over and eat at my place, or you can raid my pantry—or we can go out."

"I hate this," she said as she pulled herself together. "I shouldn't fall apart just because I've had a long, hard day." She tried to pull away, but he continued to hold her close.

"Kat, honey, you can fall apart on me anytime."

"No." She tried, again, to put some physical distance between them and almost fell out of the hammock. "I'm grateful for all your help. You're the most generous man I've ever met. But I don't want our relationship to be that way. I don't want to always be the one who needs help, who needs comforting. I know you think I'm a nut about this, but this has to be a two-way street."

"I'm willing to make it whatever kind of street you want."

She sighed. "It's impossible." She pushed herself up and out of the hammock and crossed the deck. One of the puppies chased her feet, attacking her shoelaces.

"It's challenging," he corrected her, coming up from behind and whispering in her ear. "But not impossible. You're worth the effort."

Kat tried stepping away from Ethan again, but she was right at the deck railing. "Maybe this isn't the best time for me to get involved with someone. A couple of weeks ago I said I needed to take things slowly, but maybe we should cool things altogether until I'm in a better place. It's hard for me to devote time to a relationship, when I'm still in survival mode."

"So you want to wait until your life calms down?"

Did she?

"Kat, no one's life really calms down. You always think it's going to, but it doesn't. And you keep putting plans off—that dream vacation, taking up a hobby, having a relationship—until pretty soon you're old and you haven't done any of the things you wanted to do. If you keep putting your life off until tomorrow, pretty soon you've got nothing but a whole pile of dreams you always wanted to realize, but didn't."

Darn it, he was right. Should she shy away from a good man because the relationship was challenging? That seemed stupid.

Resigning herself, she leaned back against him. "You're too smart for me."

"Nah, I'm just irresistible." He nibbled on her earlobe, sending pleasurable shivers down her back.

The back door opened, and Jasmine and Samantha bounded out onto the deck hand-in-hand. Jasmine, with her long, coltish legs, was head and shoulders taller than Samantha, but the younger girl kept pace.

"Ms. Holiday," Jasmine said in her most polite voice, "can Samantha sleep over?"

Kat felt a momentary panic. Samantha had never managed a sleepover before. The one time she'd tried it, she'd been in tears at ten and had wanted to come home. But that had been last fall, and Sam had matured some since then.

Kat tried to gauge whether her daughter was in favor of this plan—or whether it was all Jasmine.

"Please, Mom?" Samantha said, answering that question. "I can go get my toothbrush and come right back."

"She doesn't even have to do that," Jasmine said. "My dad always keeps extra toothbrushes around. And she can borrow a nightgown from me. My dad says it's okay."

"C'mon, Mom," Ethan said. "Don't be a wet blanket."

Kat cast him a withering look that told him she didn't like her maternal authority being usurped. "Okay," she said, with misgivings, and both girls cheered. "But Samantha, I need a word with you."

Samantha looked a little wary, but she took Kat's hand and allowed herself to be led to the other side of the deck. They sat on a built-in wood bench.

"You sure about this?" Kat asked.

Samantha nodded enthusiastically. "Jasmine has the best collection of Barbies I ever saw. And she's nice to me. Most of the girls at school won't even *talk* to first-graders. She said she always wanted a sister."

"That's very sweet of her. You'll be extra special good?"

"Mmm-hmm."

"You called me Mom, a minute ago, instead of Mommy," Kat said. "What's up with that?"

"Jasmine calls her mother Mom. Only babies say Mommy. I want to call you Mom."

Her little girl was growing up. Kat wanted to scream no, no, no! "Okay. You *are* getting very grown up."

She sent Samantha on her way, and the two friends ran back into the house giggling.

"It's good to hear her laughing again," she said to Ethan. "When I was a kid, I never did sleepovers."

"Why not?"

She shrugged. "No one asked me. And I sure wasn't going to ask someone over to my place."

"It's too bad you missed out on that. But sleepovers are even more fun now," Ethan said. "We could have one of our own, you know."

Kat looked a bit startled by Ethan's proposition. Even though she had to have known it was coming. He'd made his intentions abundantly clear, but he was still wary of moving too fast and scaring her away. No matter how impatient he was to take things further with her, he didn't want to go where she wasn't ready to go.

"Or…we could just watch a movie or something. Preferably one that doesn't involve animated woodland animals."

Finally, he got a laugh out of her. "I guess our dates have been pretty kid-centered so far."

"And that's fine. You have your priorities straight, and I like that. But I wouldn't mind some adult time.

"Even if it's just watching TV. Even if you don't want to spend the night."

She took his hand. "I want that, too. Maybe we can pretend, for the evening, that I'm not psycho."

He clasped his hands at the back of her neck and leaned down until their foreheads touched. "You're not psycho. You're going through some adjustments, that's all. You'll come out on the other side and you'll be just fine."

"That's the thing, though, Ethan. Maybe I am going through some adjustments, but I was confused about men before the fire. I'm confused about when it's okay to lean on a man, when it's okay to let myself be taken care of, and when it's not. Where's the line that I shouldn't cross, if I don't want to be weak and whiny and clingy?"

"Trust me, you're not any of those things. I've never seen anyone so determined to handle everything by herself. But didn't you tell me that you teach the Strong-Girls teamwork?"

"Well, yeah, I do."

"So how about we're a team? And we work together on things. We help each other."

"What could you possibly need help with?"

"Well, now that you mention it—I'm into my paramedic training and, frankly, it's kicking my butt. Book learning isn't my greatest strength. But you're smart. You have a master's degree. You could help me study."

Kat was taken with the idea. "I would love to help you study. But you aren't just making this up so I'll feel useful, are you?"

He pulled her against him. "I have to memorize, like, four hundred body parts by Monday. I could start with yours."

Chapter Ten

Ethan's DVD library was heavy on action movies, but that was fine. Anything more "serious" would have required too much emotional involvement. They found a Nicolas Cage movie, curled up on the sofa and watched in contented silence.

"I think this is the first time I've actually relaxed since the fire," Kat said. "Thanks."

She kept thinking about the anatomy lesson. Ethan probably had no idea what fantasies he'd launched with that offhand comment. But as Nic Cage blew up one car after another, Kat's mind was on other things. Clavicles and quadriceps and—what was that little hollow at the base of the neck called?

She knew now, without a doubt, that she wanted to make love with Ethan. But after the movie ended, he seemed content to hold her. He probably figured he'd pushed enough, and now it was her turn.

She turned to face him, clasping her hands behind his neck just as he'd done to her earlier. "What's that little hollow place at the base of the neck called?"

A slow grin spread cross his face. "You mean this one?" He leaned in and teased the place in question with his tongue. "I don't know. But this muscle right here—" he kissed his way up to below her ear "—is the sterno-cleidomastoid."

The way he said it sounded remarkably sexy. Kat's body tingled from her hair to her toes.

"And this right here—" He circled her lips with his index finger "—is the oribicularis oris. I think. But maybe I need to investigate further."

Finally he kissed her, and she wondered why she'd ever hesitated. This felt so right. There was no longer any hesitation on her part.

It was a marathon kiss, not a fast, hot sprint but a slow, leisurely exploration, progressing from mile marker to mile marker at its own pace, changing subtly as their body chemistry churned and their blood grew warm and heavy.

Kat had goose bumps. She could feel the electricity starting in her arms and moving up to her shoulders and along her spine, traveling in waves across her hips and down her legs. She was one giant ball of pure sensation.

And for once, she wasn't cautioning herself to stop, slow down, think things through. This felt so perfect, and Ethan's bedroom was literally steps away, just down the hall, the door open and a light burning invitingly.

She rubbed against him like a needy cat. "Make love to me, Ethan."

"You're sure?"

"Yes." She was tired of thinking and scheming and planning, always weighing her options and choosing the most sensible path. She wanted to let her worries go and just feel without thinking, judging, analyzing and evaluating.

She did have at least one functioning brain cell, however: "Ethan, I don't have any birth control."

"I do." He nibbled her ear, sending a fresh wave of shivers coursing down her backbone.

It took them five minutes to actually make it to the bedroom, as they simply couldn't stop kissing. This was the one room in the house Kat hadn't seen before, and she was only dimly aware of the dimensions, white walls contrasting starkly with dark furniture.

A king-size bed. A ceiling fan, turning gently. Old-style Venetian blinds at the large double window.

Ethan pulled the covers aside and drew her down onto the bed. It was so soft. Maybe she'd grown used to her hard-as-a-rock futon, but this was like resting on rose petals.

Kat kicked off her shoes and was keen to shed her clothes, as well, but Ethan seemed in no hurry. He somehow managed to convey that he was out of his mind with lust, but patient and not wanting to rush, and she instinctively knew that no matter how eager he was for Kat, his priority would be to make her comfortable, to make her feel amazing.

He obviously didn't know that he'd achieved his goal within the first ten seconds of kissing her neck. What she didn't know, but what she was coming to find out, was that that was only the beginning. The way he touched her just so, fingertips dancing along her back, his tongue teasing the cleft in her throat, had her nearly coming out of her skin. She wanted to moan, but she controlled the urge—until she remembered they were alone in the house.

She didn't have to control herself. She didn't have to worry about anything.

She moaned. She sighed. She even *squeaked* with approval, when he found just the right spot.

Oh, the place behind her knee. She hadn't known about that one. She realized she'd somehow managed to lose most of her clothes, but she didn't remember how she'd gotten clear of them.

Now that was talent.

She made minor attempts to return the pleasure he was bestowing on her, but her brain had short-circuited long ago.

"Just relax," he said, over and over. "Let your mind go blank and enjoy yourself."

She took him at his word but couldn't help doing some of the touching, because she wanted to feel him everywhere, all around her and inside her.

Especially inside her.

He managed to sheath himself with no help from Kat, and when he finally entered her, it was as if she'd been waiting her whole life for this meeting of bodies and minds. Everything felt so right.

That goose-bump feeling started again, but this time the tingles were inside her—starting in her abdomen and spreading in a tide of pure pleasure, radiating from her fingers and toes until she was sure she must be glowing.

Each thrust from Ethan brought another level of pleasure, and she thought she could happily live the rest of her life like this, joined with him.

Finally she rose above the crest of the wave, and she had to put one hand to her mouth to stifle the screams of ecstasy that erupted. Ethan actually grinned, then turned serious as his own peak came.

They lay together for a long time, with just the hum of the ceiling fan in the background, their skin rimed with sweat. For minutes after her climax Kat experienced more small waves of pleasure washing over her, until they finally dissipated, leaving a soft halo of satisfaction in their wake.

Gradually Ethan's breathing returned to normal, and he slid off to the side. Neither of them spoke for a long time. No words were necessary, and to talk of what had passed between them would diminish their closeness, somehow.

After a while, Ethan leaned on his elbow and played with Kat's hair.

"You know what?" she asked.

"What?" he said warily.

"I have *got* to get a more comfortable bed."

He grinned. "You can use this one anytime you want."

ETHAN SLEPT surprisingly hard, given the fact the most arresting creature on earth was nestled in his arms. But sleep he did, waking only as the first light of dawn showed gray through the windows.

He lay still for a while, watching Kat sleep, her face relaxed for once. She worried too much. If he had his way, Kat Holiday would never have to worry about anything ever again. But he wasn't completely oblivious. That way of thinking wasn't going to win him her heart.

He had to go. He was on duty today, and he wished to hell he hadn't agreed to trade shifts with someone who wanted an extra vacation day this week. But he tried to be amenable when Captain Campeon made a schedule request. And the captain always asked one of the rookies first.

Ethan debated about whether to wake Kat, then decided she probably needed the sleep. He didn't think their "morning after" would be awkward, but this way he avoided the possibility. He would be really unhappy if Kat felt any regrets about the passion they'd shared.

He left her a note—and his car keys, in case she wanted to borrow his SUV. He started to leave her some money, in case she wanted to buy groceries, then decided that was pushing it. He wasn't completely uneducable. Instead, he told her to raid his fridge if she felt so inclined, and left it at that. She was smart enough not to starve herself or her daughter.

TWO WEEKS LATER, on a starry, still, hot night, Kat found herself lounging in a spectacular ski boat on Lake Ray Hubbard with Ethan, Sam, and several other people she'd just met and whose names she couldn't keep straight. It was the fire department's annual Beer, Brats, Bait and Boat party. They'd water-skied and fished, stuffed themselves with charbroiled sausages, floated on rafts at the swimming beach. Now, as was the tradition, all the boats were tied together in the middle of the lake and everyone was telling stories.

Some of the stories were about fires, and Kat watched Samantha carefully to see if any of the talk bothered her. But she seemed content, and she actually nodded off before long.

Kat wouldn't have believed she could feel so relaxed and happy, herself, this soon after her devastating fire. But after the night she and Ethan had made love, things seemed to normalize.

Something tight she'd been holding inside her had loosened and floated away, and she started to believe things would be okay. Donations were up at Strong-Girls, thanks to Deb's tireless publicity and fund-raising efforts. The new group already had nine members, and both of Kat's new counselors were working out well.

She had her own little car back, good as new.

Samantha hadn't had any more serious asthma attacks. Chuck's mother was watching Sam a couple of days a week, an arrangement that pleased everyone and saved Kat daycare money. In fact, her finances were looking a lot better. She wasn't out of the woods, yet, but barring any more disasters, she would be free of debt by the end of the summer.

And then there was Ethan.

She really did help him study, quizzing him, and

sometimes Priscilla, too. She knew very little about anatomy or biology or chemistry, but she used their study guides. She devised mnemonics to help them with long memorization lists, a trick she'd relied on when she was in school.

When Ethan wasn't studying, they worked on the yard together, planting flowers and making plans for a dog run for Winnie. They took Samantha to a baseball game one night, and they went for a drive in the country. And they made love when they could.

Kat had wanted to take things slow in their relationship, but once she'd cracked open the door, slowing down the physical part was impossible. They used some restraint when Samantha was around, but when she stayed with her father or her grandmother, or when she spent the night at Jasmine's or with her other best friend, Krista, Kat was all over Ethan.

Why the heck should they slow down, when it felt so good and wasn't harming anyone?

It was all idyllic, and Kat tried not to question her good fortune too closely. Her life had never felt so normal.

Ethan still did a lot of things for her without being asked, such as changing the oil in her car, rotating her tires, replacing burned-out lightbulbs. He bought her presents, too. She was constantly discovering things she needed, things she'd lost in the fire but hadn't immediately realized were missing.

They were just little things, and he seemed to get so much pleasure from surprising her. He was an unstoppable force, and she got tired of being the immovable object. So she stopped fighting his generosity. Virginia had counseled her to pick her battles, and that was exactly what she was doing.

She knew she wasn't quite living by the StrongGirl tenets she'd developed, and she felt a little uneasy about it. Most of the girls in her program didn't have people in their lives to take care of things for them. She was coming to depend on Ethan; she was finding it easier these days to let him do things for her.

And anytime she felt tempted to change the status quo, she quickly found herself thinking about how hurt he would be if he thought she didn't fully appreciate the way he had bulldozed into her life and her heart. And she chickened out.

"You asleep?" Ethan whispered.

"No. Just very, very relaxed."

He kissed the top of her head. "That's the way it should be."

It was late when the party broke up. Samantha woke briefly when she was transferred from the boat to the dock, but once she was in Ethan's car, she fell asleep again. Kat had a hard time holding her own eyes open.

Ethan insisted on carrying Samantha up the stairs to the apartment, and Kat let him. Sam was really too big for Kat to tote around, but for Ethan it was nothing. The little girl didn't stir as Ethan carried her into the bedroom and laid her down on the twin bed.

"It's hot in here," he said. "Why don't you try out the air conditioner? Have you even turned it on yet?"

The weather had been unusually cool for May—

until today. She flipped on the switch to the unit, set it at medium and waited. It started blowing cooler air almost immediately. Then she returned to the bedroom, where Ethan was pulling off Sam's sneakers with one hand and scratching behind Bashira's ears with the other. Her heart contracted as she watched how tender he was with Sam. A lot of men wouldn't bother with a single mom or an orphan cat, but Ethan genuinely seemed to enjoy his time with Sam and Bashira.

She couldn't help thinking about how fine it would be if he didn't have to go back to his own house—if they all lived together, as a family. But then she stopped herself. It was way too soon to be thinking those thoughts. She would have to know Ethan a lot longer before she entertained any ideas of them living together.

"She's definitely down for the count," Ethan said, his words low as he came out of the bedroom. "Do you want to put her in pajamas or anything?"

"It's okay. She can sleep in her shorts."

They said their whispered good-nights at the door. Just as Ethan was about to leave, the whole apartment went dark.

"Uh-oh, looks like we've blown a fuse. Where's your flashlight?"

Kat felt her way to the futon and reached under, finding the flashlight. She had one in every room, as part of her new home safety policy.

She went down to the garage with Ethan. It was probably a good idea to watch what he did so she could do it herself, if she had this problem again. He led her to an old-fashioned fuse box and opened it. With efficient movements he replaced the blown fuse, using one of the spares he kept on a shelf nearby.

She stepped outside and looked up. "Ta-dah! Let there be light."

Then the lights went out again.

"However briefly."

"Hmm." Ethan scratched his chin. "Looks like the problem might be more serious than a fuse. And I'm on duty tomorrow. Why don't you guys bunk with me until we can get the problem solved? I can work on it Monday first thing."

"I don't want to wake Samantha up," she said. "We'll be fine for couple of nights. Soon as I open some windows and get a cross breeze going, we'll be cool enough."

Ethan was doubtful, but after Kat ran upstairs to turn off the air conditioner and Ethan replaced the fuse for a second time, she reassured him that she did not mind a little heat. She shooed him on his way. "Get some sleep. You might have to put out a fire tomorrow and you'll need to be fully alert."

He left, but only reluctantly.

As Kat got ready for bed, she noticed that her answering machine had a message. She pushed the button and listened as she undressed.

"Hi, Kathryn, this is Sandy Taylor at White Cliffs. A nice corner unit has come available. It's ready immediately. So if you're still interested, give me a call." And she rattled off the number.

White Cliffs. The nice, new town houses over near Bishop Arts. She'd left her name and number when she'd first been apartment hunting. The units were spacious, modern and beautiful, and the rent was reasonable—and they accepted small pets. But there hadn't been a vacancy.

Now there was.

And yet the thought of moving again had little appeal. Samantha was just getting settled here and Kat hated to uproot her. Though the garage apartment was tiny, they were managing—enjoying themselves, even. And with the minuscule rent Ethan was charging, she could get back on her feet quicker.

Kat thought about it for all of five more seconds, then erased the message.

WHEN ETHAN CAME HOME from his shift early Monday morning, he wanted nothing more than to dive into bed. He'd gotten almost no sleep the previous night, since he'd been on watch command and the alarms had come in one after another after another. But he wanted to take a closer look at Kat's fuse box and the whole wiring situation. If it was what he suspected… Ouch.

Kat must have heard him rummaging around in the garage, because she showed up at the door a couple of minutes later wearing a pale green suit.

He couldn't help smiling when he saw her, fresh and green as a new tomato on the vine. "You look so businesslike. But all girl."

She beamed a smile at him. "Thanks. I've got an important meeting this morning, so I borrowed the suit from Deb. I haven't really had time to replace my business wardrobe yet. I'm leaving now, but I wanted to say thank you for getting on this problem right away."

He shrugged. "I'd be a crummy landlord if I let it slide. Where's Samantha?"

"She's at her dad's. I have to confess, she bailed out on me. It was too hot. But Chuck's been traveling a lot lately and hasn't gotten to spend much time with her, so it's fine."

"Well, with luck your place will be cooler when you get home tonight."

Thirty minutes later, he realized he'd been way too optimistic. He couldn't believe he'd made such a tactical error.

The current fuse box wasn't sufficient to support the power pull of an air conditioner—especially the large one he'd installed. He was going to have to put in an updated breaker box, and that wasn't a short-term project. Plus, he was up to his ears in paramedic training. He wouldn't have time to complete the rewiring for at least a week, not if he didn't want to flunk out.

He could hire an electrician, but that would cost a fortune.

Then, a wonderful idea occurred to him. Instead of cursing his lack of foresight, he started to feel fortunate to have such a problem.

Chapter Eleven

Later that day, after Kat got home from work, Ethan walked across the yard to her apartment, where he found the door open. Inside, Kat was busily opening every window in the place. It was stifling! She definitely couldn't stay here for the week or two it would take to complete the wiring.

She noticed him standing there, and a worried expression crossed her face. "I guess the problem isn't fixed yet, huh?"

"No, it's not." And he delivered the bad news. "I know how to fix it, but it's gonna to take some time. A week, maybe two. I could hire an electrician—"

"Oh, no, that would cost a fortune. You can just do it when you have time. A little heat won't kill us, and it's just for a couple of weeks."

"Kat, you'll die of heat stroke if you stay here. But you don't have to roast. You can stay with me." He threw the suggestion out casually. "Sam can sleep in the room upstairs, and you can use the third bedroom for—"

"Whoa, whoa, whoa," she said, holding out her hand

like a traffic cop stopping cars. "I don't think this is such a good idea."

"Why not?"

"It wouldn't be proper. I mean, it wouldn't be a good example to set for Samantha."

"You mean because we're not, like, married?"

She nodded. "I know it's old-fashioned. And I'm not totally against couples living together, but we're not exactly…" She struggled for a word.

"Committed?"

"Well, yeah, I guess. We've been seeing each other a very short time."

"It would only be a temporary arrangement," he reasoned. "Just until I can get the wiring fixed and the A/C working."

Kat was already shaking her head before he finished his sentence. "Really, not a good idea," she said with steely determination.

"Kat, don't rule it out before you've thought about it. Do you really want Sam to be away for two weeks while you're without A/C?"

"No, I don't. But I can't move in with my boyfriend," she said with troubling finality. "That's sending the wrong message to Samantha about how to deal with challenges. And what would I tell the StrongGirls? The most important thing I can do for them is to teach them by example."

"So you'd rather roast in this oven than compromise a little?"

"I can't compromise my values. If I lose those, I lose

everything. Anyway, there's another issue." She glanced out the window, chewing on her fingernail, then turned back again. "Sam is getting way too attached to you."

"That's not a bad thing," Ethan said, confused. "It certainly beats having her scream when I walk into the room."

"But if something happens, you know, with you and me. Not that I think it will—"

"I'm not going anywhere," he said flatly.

"We don't know what the future holds. We've only known each other a little while. It's too much, too soon. And frankly, once Sam and I live a couple of weeks in your beautiful house, with that big kitchen and those roomy closets, it's not going to be easy to move back here."

Ethan had to admit, he'd been sort of counting on that. They'd get comfortable, everything would be running smoothly, so why would she want to pack up and move out?

He must not have looked convinced, because she added one more ingredient to her argument.

"When I was about Sam's age, my mother moved us in with one of her boyfriends. I mean, she did it more than once, but that particular time, the guy was nice. I remember him very clearly—his name was Hal. He was a mechanic and he smelled like motor oil—and he had a cute little house. He gave me butterscotch candies and called me Kitten. But after a few months something went wrong and we had to move away, and I never saw Hal again. I was heartbroken. And I know it's because we lived with him and he felt like a daddy to me."

"You think Samantha sees me like a daddy?" The idea filled him with wonder and pride.

"I think if we lived together, she would start to get that idea, yes."

"So you're just going to stay here and roast."

"I'll be working during the heat of the day. And it's not so bad at night. I mean, people lived for thousands of years without air-conditioning. I hardly ever had it when I was growing up."

Nothing he was going to say would dissuade her, and he had no choice but to give up. He would simply get the job finished as quickly as he could.

"Then, I better get to work while I still have some daylight. The sooner I can finish this thing, the sooner you'll be cool again."

As Kat watched him go, she felt an unreasonable urge to cry. He really did have her best interests in mind. He wanted to take care of her and Sam, and that was a noble thing. The guy's heart was as big as a beach ball.

And it was tempting—far more tempting than she'd let him know—to move into that wonderful old house, with its polished hardwood floors and high ceilings, and the funny spiral staircase that led up to the attic conversion where Samantha liked to play.

Hadn't she fantasized about it just two nights ago? If she and Ethan were further along in their relationship, if they were in love and committed to making a future together, things might be different. If that were the case, and Ethan had asked her to move in simply because he wanted to live with her, she might be okay with it.

But to shack up with her new boyfriend for convenience's sake just didn't seem right.

She had already let herself become too dependent on Ethan. Though they were, technically, living in separate residences, they might as well be living together— sharing meals, working on the yard and doing their grocery shopping together. Ethan often looked after Samantha while Kat was at work.

She'd moved into this tiny apartment as a last-resort emergency solution, and she'd allowed herself to get way too comfortable here. She'd told herself it was the best situation she could find, a rationalization that had worked for a while. But now a White Cliffs town house was available.

She'd erased the message from Sandy Taylor, but she still had the woman's business card somewhere. She dug through her purse, found the card and dialed the number before she could change her mind.

Unfortunately, Kat could only reach Sandy's voice mail, but she left a message saying that she definitely would take the apartment. Samantha wouldn't be pleased about moving away from Ethan or Winnie *or* Jasmine next door. But she would come around once she realized she would have her own room again, as well as a swimming pool, a playground and lots of other kids to play with.

This was the only sensible move she could make. Kat was grateful for the wiring crisis, because it had pushed her into doing what she ought to have done in the first place.

Sometimes she regretted being a StrongGirl.

When it grew dark and the power tools in the garage went silent, Kat sought Ethan out. If she put off telling him of her plan any longer, it would be that much harder. She brought him a glass of cold lemonade.

"I have some good news," she said. Because, damn it, it *was* good news. A few weeks earlier she would have been ecstatic to snag one of these town houses. "A woman called from the White Cliffs town houses. It's that new complex they built over in Bishop Arts—remember, I pointed them out to you a couple of weeks ago?"

Ethan, who'd been packing away his tools, went still. He looked at her intently and made a small nod.

"They've got a corner unit available. And they've got a fantastic deal running—first month free, discounted rent for a year. It's ideal, much nicer than my old place."

"You're moving." He looked so crestfallen, Kat wanted to take back what she'd just said. But she had to do the sensible, practical thing.

"Living in your garage apartment *was* only meant to be temporary," she reminded him. "If you hadn't offered it to us, I don't know what I would have done. And we've really enjoyed living here. But the place is much too small for two people and a cat."

"I know it is. And actually, the problem is worse than I thought. Some of these walls have asbestos in them."

"Oh. Then I guess the sooner we move, the better. But it's not far—only about a mile away."

"Yeah. Yeah, you're right." He took a long sip of his

lemonade. "Now I can postpone this project, which is getting huger by the minute. I've got a test to study for this week. But you'll want me to help you move, right?"

"Yes, Ethan, I would love your help." Virginia would be proud of her.

Kat was relieved he wasn't trying to talk her out of moving. But the note of resignation in his voice bothered her.

"GOOD SHOT, PRISSY!" Otis patted Priscilla on the back as she walked up to the dartboard at Brady's to retrieve her darts. "You been practicing. You still can't mop a floor worth beans, but the dart game is definitely improving."

Ethan was glad to see Otis and Priscilla getting along better. In fact, all three of them were starting to be accepted. It was a slow process, and there were a few holdouts who continued to offer snide comments or ignore the rookies altogether. But at least they weren't pariahs at Brady's anymore.

"Basque, you playin'?" Otis asked. "Loser buys the winner a beer."

"Hmm? Oh, yeah, sure."

Ethan took his turn and made some of the worst shots of his life, to several hoots and rude comments. "Guess it's not my night," he said, and he headed for the bar to buy Otis his Bud Light.

Priscilla followed him. "You seem a little preoccupied tonight." She was on her second glass of wine and in a loquacious mood, which only made Ethan's depression stand out more.

He shrugged.

"Everything going okay with Kat?" Priscilla asked, watching Ethan with keen interest.

It was hard to get anything past Priscilla, and he figured she would keep badgering him until he told her, so he did.

"I asked her to move in with me."

Priscilla smiled. "Cool. Unless… She didn't turn you down, did she? Her little place is cute now, but it must be cramped."

"She turned me down flat. She offered me an array of excuses, ranging from wanting to maintain her independence to not wanting Samantha to get the wrong idea. But the fact is, she just doesn't want to get that serious. I do and she doesn't, and I don't know what to do about it."

"Be patient, for starters. Who knows how bad she's been burned in the past? She's entitled to be cautious."

"I haven't told you the worst of it. She's found another apartment, some place bigger, with a pool, and she's moving away."

"Oh, Ethan. I'm sorry. I know you liked having Kat and Sam right there. But it's not the end of the world. I mean, you're not breaking up or anything, are you?"

"No." But he was afraid that was coming next.

She nudged him. "Then stop borrowing trouble. Hey, the shuffleboard table is free. Want to challenge…" She trailed off mid-sentence as her gaze focused on something behind Ethan. He turned to see a group of guys enter, shirt sleeves rolled up, ties askew or missing altogether.

One of the guys was Roark Epperson. He'd been in the news a lot lately as the pressure increased to catch the serial arsonist.

No wonder Priscilla was staring. At the fire academy she'd been enthralled by the subject of arson and eager to learn everything she could about how to spot suspicious fires, how the evidence was gathered. He wouldn't be surprised if some day she became an arson investigator herself.

Ethan grabbed Otis's beer and left a fiver on the bar. "Let's go get the shuffleboard table before those guys grab it."

"Uh, I think I better get home," Priscilla said suddenly. "It's late."

Ethan looked at his watch. "It's just eight-thirty." They'd spent half the afternoon studying together, and they both felt confident they'd pass tomorrow's test, so he didn't think it was that.

"I have to do laundry. And you know how long that takes me." She paid her bar tab and cleared out without another word.

That was strange.

Ethan decided to do the networking thing, which was better than sitting on the barstool alone drowning his sorrows. He walked up to Roark Epperson, held out his hand and introduced himself. "I was in the last class at the fire academy," he said.

"Oh, yeah, I remember you. You used to do construction. That's a helpful skill in arson investigation. Where'd your friend go?"

"My friend?"

"The woman who lit out of here like the Four Horsemen of the Apocalypse were chasing her. Priscilla."

"You know her?"

"There was only one woman in your class. Hard not to notice her."

"Anybody would notice her," one of Roark's friends said, elbowing a buddy. "If you know what I mean."

Roark gave his friend a shriveling look that shut him up. All of which made Ethan wonder if there was something he didn't know. Did the arson specialist and Priscilla know each other?

"I was just about to see if I could get a shuffleboard game up," Ethan said. "Any of you guys interested?"

A couple of them were, so they formed teams and went to it.

Ethan lined up to make his next play. "Any progress on catching the arsonist?" he asked Epperson, then pulled off a particularly good shot that had his opponents groaning.

"Precious little. That abandoned gas station that burned over on Ledbetter a couple of weeks ago? That was him. He'd planted a homemade bomb inside, but luckily it didn't go off."

Ethan hadn't heard about the bomb. "He's trying to kill firefighters." What a grim realization.

"Looks that way."

"Could he be a former firefighter? Someone who was fired from the department, disgruntled?" It was an unfortunate fact of life that many arsonists were, in fact, also firefighters. Sometimes they were just bored and wanted to create some action. But sometimes their motives were darker.

"That's exactly the direction I've been looking, but so far nothing's panned out." Epperson looked deeply troubled, and Ethan felt bad for bringing up the subject. The investigator had probably come to Brady's so he could forget work for a few hours.

"Your shot," Ethan said. "We can cinch it with this one."

They won, and as a team they played and beat all comers, including Tony, who'd spent most of the evening flirting with one siren sister after another.

"You da man," Tony said, acknowledging his defeat. "Hey, I'm going home. You gonna hang out here a while?"

"Home?" Ethan looked at his watch and was surprised to find it was after midnight. Where had the evening gone?

"Hey, how come you're not out with Kat?" Tony asked. "Is it mother-daughter bonding night?"

"Something like that." Although not much like that. The truth was, Ethan hadn't called her. He needed some time to process the fact that not only did she not want to move in with him, she wanted to move farther away—despite the desire that seared the air between them and the obvious logic of the arrangement.

The fact was, Ethan was way more into this relationship than Kat. Everything was out of balance. He was acting like Tony did whenever he fell for a girl, preoccupied to the point of obsession with Kat, her daughter, her life. While Kat was thinking about other things.

He knew Kat felt *something* for him. It wasn't completely one-sided on his part. But he had to ask himself whether he wanted to continue putting all his energy into the relationship when Kat sometimes seemed so ambivalent.

He settled up with Brady Keller, the original owner's grandson and a fixture behind the bar since before Ethan was born, and he and Tony walked the two blocks back to their homes.

On the way, Ethan asked Tony something he'd been wondering about. "Once you've fallen for a woman, is there any way to pull back, to not quite care so much? It'd be really nice if I could be happy with seeing Kat once or twice a week. Is there any way to get a woman out of your head once she's there?"

Tony laughed. "I bet you're feeling real sorry right now for all those times you razzed me when I had it bad."

"Actually, I do. I thought you were being melodramatic. I never knew how good—and how bad—it felt."

"Well, my friend, the only way I know of to get a woman out of your head is to meet another one."

"I don't want to meet another one. She's it. She's the one I'm going to… Oh, my God, I sound just like you."

"You'll survive. I always do. She didn't dump you, did she?"

"No. Nothing's really changed." But it had. Something had definitely changed.

KAT LAY ON HER FUTON later that night, sweating like a racehorse. Temperatures had climbed to the mid-nineties during the day. And tomorrow the forecast was for even warmer weather.

She wondered how quickly she would be able to arrange the move to White Cliffs. Except that Sandy Taylor hadn't called back despite Kat having left several messages, and Kat was getting a bit worried that the town house wasn't nailed down after all.

When she went to work the next day she was listless from the heat and lack of sleep. She would be checking up on one of the new StrongGirls groups today, observing how her new counselor was conducting herself. She also had a meeting with her own Kimball High group and a couple of one-on-one counseling sessions.

So she drank three cups of coffee while returning phone calls and tried to pull herself together.

Virginia stopped in for some brochures and stuck her head into Kat's closet-sized office. "Got a minute?" Then her forehead creased with concern. "Oh, hon, you look so tired. You're not coming down with something, are you?"

"I didn't sleep well last night," Kat said, trying for a smile. "But I'm good."

"Kat?" Deb called out from the outer office. "There's a woman named Sandy Taylor on the phone. Something about an apartment? Should I tell her you're not looking—"

Kat grabbed the phone and punched a button. "Hello, Sandy? I'm so glad you called back."

"Yeah, well, I'm really so sorry, but I rented the apartment to someone else."

"You…what?"

"You didn't call back for a couple of days, and I figured you'd already found a place."

"And you don't have anything else?"

"No, I'm sorry. Maybe later in the summer."

"Okay," Kat said in small voice. "Thanks." When she hung up, Virginia was looking at her, practically vibrating with concern, and Deb had swiveled her chair around to look, as well.

"Is there a problem?"

Oh, boy. What a mess. She felt as if she were back to square one—desperately needing a place to live and not a lot of options.

But there was an option, she reminded herself. Ethan would be thrilled to have her and Samantha move in. He wasn't going to like her conditions, though.

Chapter Twelve

Ethan whistled as he swept the last of the dirt out of Kat's future office. She hadn't, for sure, said, *yes, we're moving in,* but she'd said she wanted to talk about it. She was coming over after she finished work for the day, and he planned to show off his house to its best advantage. He'd moved his weight machine and some other junk out to the garage. He'd touched up the pale green paint, then scoured the windows and dusted the miniblinds.

It wasn't the largest of the three bedrooms, but it was nice. She would get morning sun, diffused by the big pear tree outside.

He'd also cleaned the master bathroom—he was an expert now at scrubbing grout. His mom was a stickler for bathrooms so clean you could perform surgery in them, and he'd found most women felt the same.

Kat arrived at about four, looking so somber it scared Ethan.

"Hey, nothing can be that bad," he said, taking the covered plate she'd brought in with her. "What's this?"

He peeked under the foil and saw the ugliest, lumpiest cookies in the world.

"I'm teaching the StrongGirls how to cook nutritious, cheap, quick food—something I'm a master at," she said. "I believe good nutrition is so key to feeling good and having a clear mind. But then we did cookies, just for fun. They look horrid, but they taste pretty good."

He tried one. "Mmm, not bad. Hey, let me show you your office. You'll love it."

"I already love it," she said. "I love this house and the big kitchen, and the deck and the fireplace. You don't have to sell me on how great this place is. I loved it the moment I saw it, that first day when I came to get Bashira from you."

"So are you going to do it?" he asked point-blank, unable to stand the suspense anymore.

"Yes. This is the only sane choice."

Ethan couldn't contain himself. He grabbed her and swung her around until they were both dizzy and he finally got some laughter out of her.

"Ethan, put me down."

"All right, but only if you stop frowning. It's going to be all right. I know moving is a hassle, but you've got lots of help and support lined up. We'll make it fun for you."

"I know. But, Ethan, there's something we need to discuss."

"Plenty of time for discussing anything you want." And he nuzzled her neck and kissed her ear.

She tried to duck away, but he held her fast. "No, you don't. It's time for us to celebrate. The whole time I was fixing up your home office, I kept picturing you in it. Now you're here."

"But Ethan—"

He silenced her with a kiss, and then another kiss. And every time he stopped to take in a gasping breath, and she looked as if she were going to start talking again, he just kissed her with that much more determination. Knowing her, she wanted to discuss rent and how to share the utility costs, or who was going to be responsible for cleaning the kitchen. Whatever practical problems she had could just wait.

He wanted her here and now, under his roof, in his bed.

"What about—" she began, but he overruled her.

"Sam's safe and sound at her father's house." He knew Samantha's schedule almost better than Kat did. He unbuttoned her blouse enough that he could kiss the tops of her full breasts, unfastening the front clasp of her bra and teasing one nipple with his tongue in a way that was sure to short-circuit her brain and curtail rational thought. He'd had some practice, now. He knew exactly what buttons to push.

She moaned low in her throat. "This isn't fair."

"I'm not trying to be fair." He scooped her up in his arms and carried her to the master bedroom where his big pillow-top bed with fresh sheets awaited them.

Kat knew this was wrong. After she issued her ultimatum, Ethan might not want her to move in. He might not want her in his house *or* in his bed. He might want to wash his hands of her altogether.

She supposed that was why she was allowing it to

happen. She wanted this—she needed this. Because it might very well be the last time. Besides, Ethan was playing dirty pool. He knew she had no power to resist when he did that neck-nuzzling thing, and then the nipple thing with his tongue. The only way to stop the freight train of their mutual passion was for her to get mad, and that wasn't going to happen—not when he'd just opened up his home to her.

She was surprised when Ethan slowed his sensual assault. "Kat. I'm sorry, I'm being pushy again. If you'd rather not make love right now, it's okay."

He'd given her the perfect escape route. But did she use it? She looked him square in his passion-glazed eyes and finished unbuttoning her blouse, her intentions clear. She was simply out of willpower.

Ethan's bed was like a cloud, with its sunshine-smelling sheets and the ceiling fan blowing a cool breeze against her heated skin. She let herself give in to every feeling her body offered as Ethan removed the rest of her clothes.

When she was naked, he paused and just gazed at her. "You're the most beautiful woman I've ever seen." His voice was rough with emotion.

Oh, God. Why did he have to be so tender? Why couldn't he be fast and rough, and make her glad this would be the last time? Her chest tightened and her throat constricted. "Please, Ethan. Please hurry. Make love to me." She wouldn't be able to bear it if he took all after-noon—which she knew he was perfectly capable of doing.

At her words, his eyes seemed to burn into her, and

a new intensity filled him. He practically ripped off his own clothes, peeling his T-shirt over his head and shedding his shorts and briefs in one economical motion.

She'd seen him naked a few times now. Still, the sight of his body moved her all over again. He was so perfect, so strong and hard, his arousal drawing her focus.

Something inside her leapt at the anticipation of having him, as if this were the first time instead of the last. She drew him down and touched him, encircling him with her fingers.

Now it was his turn to groan. "What are you doing, Kat?"

"I just… I don't know. I want to touch all of you and feel you all over me."

He leaned across her and kissed her, and it was a first kiss all over again. "That can be arranged," he whispered.

She thought he would enter her then, but instead he kissed and suckled her breasts while his hand delved between her legs, where she was hot and slick and swollen with desire. She was perfectly ready for him, but still he didn't enter her.

Instead he kissed her…there. He'd done it before, pleasured her in this way, but he'd never drawn her into such a state of frenzied readiness before. She was truly mindless now and glad of it; there were times when thinking was a detriment, and this was one of them.

In moments, he had her writhing, begging him to give her some relief, which he did by quickly moving up and plunging into her. Every nerve ending in her body expressed its approval in a cataclysmic climax. Then she rode the crest of a long, long wave, as Ethan kept moving, again and again and again.

When Ethan reached his climax and the whole extraordinary episode finally reached its dénouement, Kat could hardly believe anything like that was possible. And the tenderness that followed was just too much.

She burst into tears.

"Kat, are you… What's wrong?"

"You wouldn't let me tell you before," she said, now feeling as utterly miserable as she'd felt wonderful a few moments ago.

"You're right, I wouldn't, but the delay was worth it, wasn't it? Kat?" He grabbed a tissue from his nightstand and gently blotted her tears. "I'm listening now."

"After I tell you, you're not going to want me to move in at all."

"That's ridiculous. You could confess you're an ax murderer, and I'd still want you to move in. I'd rehabilitate you."

She sighed, getting herself back under control. "Even if I need to break up with you?"

"What?" Ethan tugged his ear, as if he thought his hearing might be going.

Kat sat up, putting some distance between them. She wrapped the sheet protectively around herself and climbed all the way out of bed. He reached out to stop her, but in his post-sex lethargy, he was too slow.

"I can't let my *boyfriend* rescue me from an uncomfortable situation," she said. "That goes directly against who I am and everything I stand for. If I move in here, it's strictly as a housemate. I'll move my things into that pretty green bedroom, and I want to pay you a fair and reasonable rent, just as if I were any person off the street—someone who'd answered an ad in the paper."

"Kat, you don't have to…"

"Yes, I do. If you don't agree to those terms, I can't move in."

Ethan could not believe she was doing this. Everything was going so great. Why did she want to ruin it?

He'd been fantasizing about having Kat here every day when he woke up. Fixing meals together. Talking things over. Putting Samantha to bed each night and then making love.

Now she'd given him an untenable choice. Break up with her, or have her move far away.

"I don't understand you, Kat," he finally said. "I've never been so happy as these past couple of weeks, and you've seemed happy, too. Why do you want to spoil it?"

"I have been happy," she agreed as she hunted about the room for her clothes. "You've been fantastic with me and Samantha. But I can't live with myself, if I let you bail me out. Again. That's just what I let Chuck do. Then I ended up married to him."

He studied her as she quickly put on her clothes, as if by staring at her he could figure her out. But she was still a puzzle to him. Her brain worked in mysterious, inexplicable ways.

"I'm not Chuck," he said.

"I know. But maybe, deep down, I'm still that orphaned seventeen-year-old. And I want to be a grown-up."

"So that's it? We don't even get to talk about this?" Ethan asked.

"I've done nothing but think about it since yesterday. I've explained my decision the best way I know how," she said in that firm, implacable way of hers, and with a sinking feeling Ethan knew he wasn't going to argue his way out of this one.

"I want you and Samantha to move in," he said. "I want you to be safe and comfortable, and I want Sam to stay with you. So I'll agree to your terms."

"And you can't try to change my mind. Because I'm weak and I'll eventually cave, and then I'll be mad at both of us."

"Fine," Ethan said tightly. "I won't try to change your mind."

"It's not forever," she said, trying to placate him. "This is a temporary solution. I *will* find a place of my own. I lost that apartment at White Cliffs because I got too complacent. But another will come along."

Yeah, and meanwhile she could find someone else to fall in love with. He decided not to mention that possibility. Why put ideas into her head?

"Ethan…"

"Yes?" He couldn't keep the frustration out of his voice.

"I shouldn't have let you seduce me like that, knowing what I had to tell you. I apologize."

That was Kat's logic. Apologizing for giving him the

most amazing sex of his life. "I didn't give you much choice," he said grudgingly. Which was part of the problem. He didn't always give her much choice. Now she was returning the favor.

With a sigh he climbed out of bed, letting go of his fantasy that they could spend the whole evening there. "When do you want to move in?"

KAT HAD KNOWN it would be hard, but she'd had no idea how hard, to keep her hands off Ethan. It started the day he helped her move in. She'd told him he didn't need to, but of course he'd overridden her and done it anyway, which was good. She'd have broken her back trying to move Samantha's bed.

He'd shown up in cut-off jeans and a paint-spattered T-shirt that molded itself to the muscles of his broad back in intriguing ways. She couldn't stop staring at the way his biceps bunched up when he lifted something heavy. And he was the only man she'd ever known who got more attractive when he was hot and sweaty, instead of less so.

She, on the other hand, looked and felt about as sexy as someone's discarded gym towel. But what did that matter? The last thing she wanted was to encourage Ethan's attraction to her. Still, she didn't have to encourage it. She saw it in his eyes. He kept to his word, saying and doing nothing the slightest bit flirtatious. He was polite and relatively pleasant, though she suspected that was mostly for Samantha's sake.

Kat missed the flirting, the winks, the long, passionate gazes that had flashed so hot she was sure they'd set off her smoke detector. At least once every five minutes she questioned whether she'd made the right decision. Then she would tell herself that Ethan had become a habit, one she would have to break, at least temporarily.

Tony, Priscilla and Jasmine all helped with the move, too, and they couldn't have been nicer. With so many helping hands, it was done quickly. But what really got to Kat was when Ethan, with Priscilla's help, rigged a canopy of sorts over Samantha's bed. They tacked lengths of pastel gauze to the ceiling, allowing it to drape and swoop and dangle in places, forming a curtain. It looked like something out of a sultan's harem.

"It's a princess bed!" Samantha and Jasmine exclaimed at the same time when they entered the room, and Kat could see the satisfaction Ethan took in Sam's surprise and joy.

Jasmine helped Sam arrange her toys on her bookshelf, and when she saw how few dolls Sam had, she'd offered up one of her prized Barbies, which Samantha had graciously agreed to "borrow" until such time as she had more Barbies of her own.

Watching the girls interact with so much thoughtfulness and consideration made the lump in Kat's throat grow bigger.

Priscilla helped Kat arrange her furniture. Hers was the smallest bedroom, but after sharing space with Samantha, it seemed luxurious.

"Mom," Samantha said, standing in Kat's doorway. "Can I go outside and play with Winnie? I put all my toys away and hung up my clothes."

"You've been a very hard worker today," Kat agreed. "You, too, Jasmine. So, yes, you may play outside, as long as you stay in the yard."

Priscilla had a funny look on her face as the girls dashed away.

"Is something wrong?" Kat asked.

"Oh, no. It's just—Samantha is so cute."

"Thank you," Kat said. "She's a handful, but I couldn't live without— Oh, shoot." She realized she was bleeding, and Priscilla saw it, too. The blood was coming from a scrape on her arm. She didn't remember hurting herself, but now that she saw the scrape, it started to smart.

"Oh, Kat, that looks nasty. Better let Ethan and me patch you up. We *have* finished two weeks of our eighteen months of paramedic training, after all."

Kat laughed as she grabbed a handful of tissues to wipe away the blood. "Hmm, maybe I better talk to Tony."

But she didn't get the chance. Ethan took one look at her arm, sat her down at the kitchen table and fussed over her little scrape as if she'd severed a limb. Meanwhile, Priscilla and Tony made themselves scarce. Ethan washed the minor injury and put antibiotic ointment on it, touching her with professional detachment.

With every stroke of his fingers on her arm, she had to stifle a small gasp of pleasure. No pain now.

"I don't know if I have a bandage big enough," he said. "But if I don't, maybe Tony has something next door."

"Ethan, you've done enough, really. This isn't your problem."

The look on his face grew fierce. "Kat. Maybe we're not a couple anymore. But I can't automatically stop caring about you. Deal with it."

"YOU GOTTA FIND another woman," Tony insisted. They were on duty hosing down the engine—for once, they hadn't been assigned to clean the bathroom.

Priscilla was also out in the front drive. She had a gas can and a lawn mower, and she was trying her best to figure out where the gas went. Captain Campeon had gotten tired of making Priscilla mop, since she did it so cheerfully no matter how bad she was at it. So he'd told her she had to mow the grass.

True to form, she wasn't complaining, nor was she asking for help. But it was clear she'd never been within ten feet of a lawn mower.

"Tony, you leave Ethan alone," she said as she stared at the lawn mower, scratching her head. She tipped it over to see if anything on the bottom looked promising. "He's in love. Women aren't interchangeable, like cars."

"Who says?" Tony shot back.

Ethan focused on a spot of dirt, scrubbing it and then polishing it until he'd about polished a hole. He couldn't join in the good-natured chatter. It hurt too much to talk about Kat, or even think about other women.

She'd been living in his house a week, and she'd been the ultimate thoughtful roommate. She'd paid her rent, contributed grocery money and done more than her share of the cleaning and cooking. She was quiet, and she made sure Samantha understood how to respect her new housemate's belongings.

"But why torture yourself when you could move on?" Tony argued. "There's a siren sister at Brady's who's dying for you to notice her."

"Uh, no, thanks." Ethan shivered at the thought. He knew the woman Tony was talking about. She had more tattoos than a sailor.

"He doesn't need to move on," said Priscilla. "He just has to wait her out. Kat thinks going platonic is the responsible thing to do. But she'll regret it. She'll change her mind."

"How do you know that?" Ethan asked, pathetically eager for any scrap of hope.

"Because she's in love with you. Any idiot can see that."

Ethan's chest tightened. "You think? Really?" Could that possibly be true? She sure didn't act like it.

"It's the way she looks at you when you're not looking." Priscilla finally settled on the oil cap and unscrewed it.

"No!" Tony and Ethan said together.

"What?"

"That's where the oil goes," Tony said. "Here's the gas cap." He unscrewed it for her.

"Oh, that thing?"

Funny, but Ethan had felt no compulsion at all to rescue Priscilla when she was having trouble. She just seemed so capable, so in control.

But Kat was one of the strongest, most capable women he'd ever known. Why, then, did he always want to take care of her? Yes, she'd been going through tough times since the fire, but she'd proved, over and over, that she could solve her own problems. If a lawn mower had baffled her, she'd have found the instruction manual or called a hardware store to get advice. She and Priscilla were alike in some ways—neither of them could bear the slightest hint that they were weaker or not as smart as a man.

But there was something so vulnerable about Kat. If someone hurt Priscilla, she had a rich family and a team of lawyers she could fall back on. If someone hurt Kat, she had no one—except him.

He was her knight in shining armor. And he liked it that way. It wasn't going to change.

"I just want to make her happy," Ethan said, almost to himself, returning to his task of drying water spots off the engine.

Priscilla abandoned her lawn mower, came over and put her arms around Ethan in a friendly hug. "Kat is the only one who can make Kat happy. But Ethan, I have a question for you, and I think you should consider it."

"Okay, what?"

"If Kat's life wasn't in such a mess, would you still be attracted? I mean, if she had lots of money and no problems and she lived in a nice house in North Dallas."

Ethan looked down at Pris. "Yes, of course I'd feel the same."

"Okay, what I'm saying is, you have a big heart and you like to help people. And maybe that's the attraction here. Tony says every girl you've ever dated has been a rescue case."

"I know." After careful scrutiny of his past loves, he'd concluded that Tony was right. "But this is different."

Their discussion had to end there, because just then the alarm sounded, and they dropped everything and ran for their turnout gear. And for the next hour, Ethan pushed all thoughts of Kat from his mind as he focused on finding the source of the smoke that a church full of people in swanky Kessler Park had suddenly started to smell during an afternoon lecture.

Tony found smoke coming out of a fluorescent light. He put out the smoldering fixture, which took all of fifteen seconds, but you'd have thought he'd rescued six people from a burning building, the way one of the church ladies was going on and on.

"That thing could have killed us," the woman said, running one perfectly manicured nail up the sleeve of Tony's coat. "I'm just in awe of what you fellas do every day. You're so brave."

"It's just our job," Tony said.

Ethan rolled his eyes and started checking the other light fixtures with a thermal imaging device, to make sure there was only one faulty one.

"My name's Daralee Ingram," the woman said.

"Antonio Veracruz," Tony said, whipping off his

helmet, and Ethan inwardly groaned. Tony had found himself a live one. In another ten minutes, he would be in love.

Ethan used to find it amusing the way his best friend could feel so intensely, so quickly about a woman he'd just met, then feel so down-in-the-dumps when the affair ended. Now, it didn't seem so funny.

After the firefighters packed their gear and headed back to the station, Ethan couldn't help but dwell on Priscilla's question. Maybe he *did* enjoy being the rescuer just a little too much. Yes, it was noble to want to help those who were weaker. But when did a guy become *too* noble? Did he truly have Kat's best interests at heart or was he trying to force her to depend on him, so she would need him?

When she'd announced she was moving to White Cliffs, he'd felt that something in their relationship had changed. Something was wrong. Now, he knew what it was. If she moved away on her own, it was proof she no longer needed him.

If she didn't need him, would he still feel the same about her? He was pretty sure he would. But the more crucial question was, would *she* feel the same?

Chapter Thirteen

"He was a creep, anyway," Tati declared. Her dream man, the one who'd claimed he wanted to marry her, had used her and dumped her, just as Kat had feared. "But I have so learned my lesson, Ms. Kat. I am not depending on any man for anything, anymore."

They were in the school cafeteria, where Kat was helping the girls fill out job applications. The group was smaller today, because some of the girls had already gotten jobs. Which was mostly good news, except that Kat missed them.

No matter what lesson they had on the agenda for the day, talk always turned to boyfriends and sex—an area Kat did not feel real confident about right now. But she did her best.

"I'm really happy to hear you say that, Tati," Kat said, beaming. "Certainly having a boyfriend can be a wonderful thing. But not if you sacrifice everything else in your life for his sake."

"Sure, it's easy for you to say that," Stephie grumbled. "You *have* a boyfriend."

Kat had probably shared more of her personal life with the girls than was prudent. But she'd discovered that when she opened up, they did, too, and that was the goal, to get an honest dialogue going.

"I *had* a boyfriend, until recently."

They gasped in unison. "Did he dump you?" Tati asked breathlessly.

"No, it was a mutual decision." Faced with skeptical hoots and out-and-out accusations that she was lying, she admitted that she was the one who ended the relationship.

"Why for?" asked Gwen, who was seventeen and the oldest member of this group. She'd really blossomed over the past few months, having gone from academic probation—almost dropping out—to decent grades. She'd even begun to talk about college.

"The relationship was too one-sided," Kat answered. "He was doing all the giving and I was doing all the taking, and it didn't feel right."

"So why didn't you start giving more back?"

"Well, I gave as much as I could. You all know about the fire, and what a difficult position I was in. But even when I tried to give him something simple, like making him a sandwich or cleaning up his kitchen, he didn't want to accept anything from me."

"Sounds like the opposite of my guy," Tati said. "My ex-guy. He just wanted to take, take, take."

"Extremes in any direction aren't good," Kat said.

"What about sex?" Stephie asked. "You can give him that. That's all most guys care about, anyway."

"We've talked about this," Kat said patiently. "Sex isn't a payment. It's a mutual sharing."

"What about love?" Tati asked softly. "If you really love each other, can't that fix everything?"

"Sometimes love can't fix everything."

"But it can sure motivate you to try to fix *some* things," Gwen said, her eyes dreamy. She'd recently met a new guy. He was twenty-two, but he owned a car wash and seemed, at least on the surface, to be a huge step up from her previous drug dealer.

"Ms. Kat?" said Stephie, and Kat braced herself for another love/sex question. But instead Stephie said, "That man is watching us again."

Kat turned, and sure enough the same silver-haired man was leaning against the cafeteria wall, arms folded, watching them. Not even pretending to be doing something else.

This was too much. She was going to find out, once and for all, why this guy was so interested in the Strong-Girls. She got up and marched toward him, full of purpose, with a bit of verbal encouragement from the girls to kick his ass.

Kat stuck out her hand and introduced herself. "Can I help you with something?" she asked, trying not to sound confrontational.

He introduced himself as James Canfield and handed her a card. "I was just observing. I'd heard about the StrongGirls program and I wanted to see for myself what you were up to."

"I appreciate your interest," Kat said carefully. "And

if you'd like to make an appointment and come to my office, I'd be happy to tell you anything you want to know about the program. But these coaching sessions are private."

"Oh, sorry," he said, immediately contrite. "I didn't mean to intrude. And I apologize for being rather…clandestine. But I was afraid if you knew you were being observed, you might act differently."

She studied his card. "You're an attorney?"

"I represent a client who might be a very good match for your program."

"And are you the one who's been talking to some of my girls?"

"Yes, I am. But I needed to see for myself what kind of effect your program was having. They were eager to talk about StrongGirls. Whatever you're doing, it's working."

"And we've only just begun," Kat said, with pride. "If you have someone you'd like to refer, please call me at the office. I can get you a brochure." She turned, intending to fetch a whole stack of brochures from her tote bag. If he dealt in family law or juvenile criminal defense, he might be a source for lots of referrals.

"No, wait," he said, "I have a brochure, thank you. I'll let you get back to your work now." And he strolled out of the cafeteria, leaving Kat baffled.

Later, as Kat was driving home, the girls' questions and opinions about love echoed in her head. Could love fix everything?

She didn't love Ethan. She hadn't allowed herself to

fall, because she'd told herself it wasn't time yet. But how could she be sure? Maybe she needed to be more flexible and take a risk.

Would it really have been a mistake to just move in with Ethan, keeping their relationship intact? She'd told herself she was protecting Samantha from hurt, but who was she really protecting?

She was going to think long and hard about her priorities and what was really important. Standing strong and being independent were all well and good, but how high a price was she willing to pay for the privilege?

"BASQUE!"

"What? Oh, sorry, Captain." Ethan had pulled KP duty and was chopping up potatoes for hash browns. If the fire department was teaching him one thing, it was how to cook.

"In my office. Now."

"Yes, sir." He quickly wiped off his hands on a dishcloth, his heart beating a hundred miles an hour. What did Campeon want with him? What had he done wrong this time? His current shift was less than an hour old, so he couldn't imagine anything he'd done that would incur the captain's wrath.

On his last shift, Ethan had been the one to spot smoke as they were driving the engine back from a false alarm, and they'd caught a young kid setting a fire in a Dumpster. Ethan had chased down the little firebug and, rather than getting tough with him, had engaged in a long discussion about the damage that could have occurred to nearby houses—and people—if the fire department hadn't happened upon the scene. The kid had been in tears afterward, and had promised not to set any more fires. He'd even expressed interest in the fire department's Explorer program.

Ethan's efforts had earned him a rare compliment from the captain.

So what was wrong?

Captain Campeon looked more nervous than Ethan felt. Not mad at all. Ethan took a chair and waited.

"Part of my job is to see that my men—and women—are fitting in and adjusting to the job. It's a sort of touchy-feely thing I'm not very good at."

"I've been hanging out at Brady's," Ethan said immediately, since Campeon had been the one to suggest it.

"I didn't bring you in here to reprimand you. You and Veracruz and Garner have gone out of your way to fit in. You've taken a lot of flak without complaint, and it's paying off. I know being a rookie isn't easy—especially not in this situation."

"I'm not complaining. I love this company," Ethan said, meaning it. Oh, God, was he about to get transferred? He'd go wherever the department wanted him, but he hated the thought of working without Tony and Priscilla by his side.

"You don't seem very happy."

Ethan was startled that the captain even noticed the moods of the firefighters under his leadership.

"I've been a little bummed because Kat and I broke up," Ethan admitted, wanting the captain to know it had nothing to do with job satisfaction. "I hadn't realized it was affecting my work."

"It's not. You're doing a good job. You're gonna go far. And I did hear about your breakup. The firefighter grapevine thrives."

Ethan was pleased with the praise—Campeon didn't often go out of his way to give pats on the head. But he was still puzzled as to why he was sitting here.

"I was sorry to hear you broke up. Kat seems nice. I thought she'd moved in with you."

"She did. *And* we broke up. It's complicated."

The captain cleared his throat, indicating he wasn't interested in any messy details. Thank God. "So, anyway. I thought you might want to meet my sister."

"Uh." Ethan was speechless. A setup? He'd never been on a blind date, and he didn't intend to start now. "She's single?" he finally asked, realizing immediately what an idiotic question it was.

"Of course, she's single!" Campeon thundered. "Would I offer to introduce you if she was married?"

"No, sir." Hell. If it was anyone else, he would quickly make it clear he wasn't interested. But this was his captain.

"She's divorced. Has a couple of kids. Her ex is a jerk—she always dates jerks.

"I want her to meet some nice, gainfully employed guys. And since I know you're unattached, and you like kids…"

"Sure, Captain, I'd love to meet your sister." What else could he say?

"Great. We're having a big barbecue here on the Fourth of July. Friends and family invited. That would be a good time for you to meet Tina and her kids, don't you think?"

Ethan nodded. "Sure." Oh, Lord, what a nightmare. Not only did he have a blind date, but he'd have to conduct it with Captain Campeon watching. Not to be insensitive, but if she were unattractive or if she hated him on sight, he would never live it down. He would be the butt of fire-department jokes for years to come.

"In case you're wondering, she's a former runner-up Miss Latina Texas. But I appreciate your saying yes even before seeing her picture." He pulled a picture out of the drawer, and Ethan studied it.

Tina was, indeed, a babe.

Ethan hadn't given up totally on Kat. But they were broken up for now, and maybe spending time with another woman would ease the pain—or at least help to pass the time. He tried to feel some optimism about meeting Tina, about moving forward. But he felt nothing.

To Kat's surprise, James Canfield, the lawyer who'd been so interested in StrongGirls, called her the day after talking with her at the Sunset High cafeteria. His client, he said, was Oscar Breckenridge. He paused, waiting for her reaction. But while the name sounded familiar, it meant nothing to her.

"Yes, well," Canfield said, "Mr. Breckenridge is most anxious to meet with you."

"Does he have a daughter who could benefit from the program?" Kat asked, a bit confused.

Canfield laughed. "No, no. I'm afraid I haven't made myself clear. He's interested in helping you with the StrongGirls program. He's impressed with it, but he can see that you're underfinanced."

"So he'd like to make a donation?"

"Something like that. He'll explain it all to you himself. He'd like to meet with you tomorrow morning at eight a.m. Now, I know that's very short notice and I'll understand if you're already committed, but his schedule is very tight."

Kat flipped her calendar to the next day. "As it happens, I don't have anything scheduled. Would he like to meet here?"

"He wants to meet at his office downtown. Parking is difficult and expensive, so he'll send a car to pick you up."

Well, this *was* nice.

Since the meeting was early, it didn't make sense for Kat to come into the office first, so she gave Mr. Canfield her home address and said she could be picked up there.

THE NEXT MORNING, as she rushed out of her bedroom, her arms loaded with StrongGirls materials, she ran smack into Ethan.

"Oh, sorry," she said breathlessly as he steadied her. She'd overslept by a few minutes, waking only when Sam's grandmother called, announcing she had come down with a cold and couldn't watch her granddaughter that day as planned. "Ethan, I need a huge favor. Can you watch Sam for a couple of hours this morning? My babysitter fell through."

"I'd be happy to," he said, "and it isn't a huge favor. But where are you off to so early?"

"A taxi is picking me up in…" She consulted her watch. "Yipes. Five minutes. Someone may actually want to invest in the StrongGirls program. Oh, Ethan, I'm so excited. Maybe I can get this guy to underwrite printing the StrongGirl book."

"You wrote a book?" he asked, taking the heavy box of materials out of her arms and carrying it toward the front door.

"It's more of a course manual, with worksheets and exercises and little inspirational essays. But right now I photocopy everything and stick it in a binder. It's not very professional. There's a copy in that box, if you want to see."

Ethan seemed more interested in talking than reading. "But you *could* write a book," Ethan said. "One of those motivational kinds that shoot straight up to number one on the bestseller list."

"Don't tempt me! As if I don't have enough to do." She looked down and saw she had a spot on her blouse. "Oh, no. Ethan, would you look out and see if the taxi is here, please? And if it is, tell the driver I'm coming. I've got to change shirts."

She didn't wait to see if he agreed. She dropped the box, her tote bag and her briefcase at the door and ran back to her room, mentally going through her closet and wondering if there was *anything* else presentable.

She found a silk shell that was only slightly wrinkled and put it on. Though it was too hot for a jacket, she grabbed one anyway. Better hot than wrinkled-looking.

As she raced back toward the front door, she saw Ethan at the open door, smirking at her.

"What?"

"Your transportation is here. Only it's not a taxi."

She'd take an oxcart if it meant getting to meet with a possible StrongGirls benefactor. She grabbed her purse, briefcase, box and tote bag, somehow juggling them all as she headed out onto the front porch. And then she nearly dropped everything. A black stretch limousine was parked at the curb, with a uniformed driver standing next to the back door, preparing to open it for her. A couple of the neighbors were standing on their porches gawking.

"Oh, my God."

Ethan came up behind her. "I bet you'll get your book printed. Now go to your meeting. Knock 'em dead."

"Thank you. Sam's probably still asleep. Will you tell her I'll be back soon?" She gave him a quick kiss on the cheek, then ran to the limousine and climbed in, less than elegantly.

Kat tried to collect her thoughts as the limousine whisked her through the Dallas streets. But this was just too weird.

She opened the door in the glass panel between herself and the driver. "Excuse me."

"Yes, ma'am?"

"Do you work for Mr. Breckenridge?"

"Yes, ma'am."

"For how long?"

"Seven years come August."

"Does he make a habit of picking up single women and having them delivered to his door?"

The driver laughed. "No, ma'am."

"Okay, thanks." She probably should have asked a few more questions of the attorney before proceeding with this adventure. But she was into it now, and she might as well enjoy the ride. She watched the neighborhoods change from the stately frame houses of the historic district to the workaday businesses of Davis Street, through the up-and-coming Kidd Springs neighborhood and upscale Kessler Park.

Then finally, they crossed the Trinity River out of Oak Cliff and into downtown Dallas.

The limo had a small refrigerator filled with drinks and snacks. Kat's stomach was too tied up in knots to try anything. But she could get used to this. She could get used to not worrying about traffic. She could put a CD in the stereo, sit back and enjoy a few minutes of calm, as her limo whisked her along.

The limo pulled up in front of Willowplace Tower, a modern, green-mirrored skyscraper, offering some of the priciest office space in the city. One had to have permission to even get past the receptionist to the elevators.

Kat was expected, she soon discovered. A woman from Mr. Breckenridge's office came down to escort her.

Kat had never seen anything like this. The elevator was the biggest she'd ever ridden in. It even had its own sofa.

The elevator stopped on the ninth floor, and the woman, whose name was Patricia, told her the Breckenridge Foundation occupied the ninth, tenth and fourteenth floors.

"It must be a really big operation," Kat said inanely.

She'd tried to do some research on Oscar Breckenridge the night before, but the man kept a very low profile. Neither Deb nor Virginia had heard of him, and all Kat could discover was that he ran a foundation that concerned itself with doing good deeds.

The foundation's reception area had its own waterfall. Not just a fountain, but a built-in rock wall with water gushing and cascading down its surface into a pond.

The pond was full of big orange fish.

The receptionist was a woman who would have looked perfectly at home attending the symphony or giving a garden party. She was of indeterminate age and the epitome of culture and good taste.

"Ms. Holiday," she said with a smile of genuine warmth. "Mr. Breckenridge is waiting for you."

"I'll take her back," Patricia said.

Kat felt a panic attack coming on, as she was led down a series of carpeted hallways that all said Money. Everything from the antique oil paintings on the walls to the inch-thick wool carpet said this place meant serious business.

What was she doing here, with her discount-store

suit and her stubby fingernails? Everyone she saw was so polished.

Patricia tapped gently on a door that was cracked open, and at the hearty, "Come on in!" she opened it wide and gave Kat a little push inside.

"Kat Holiday." The man behind the desk was smaller than average, with a silver crew cut and big black-framed glasses. He stood to greet her with a wide, re-assuring smile, his hand outstretched. "I've been looking forward to finally meeting you face-to-face."

Kat stepped forward on shaky legs. "I'm afraid you have the advantage."

"Please, sit down. And I'll tell you who I am. And then I'll tell you what I want to do for you."

And he did. As Kat sipped from a glass of cold water that Patricia had brought for her, Oscar Breckenridge told her how he'd grown up with nothing, and how a man from the Big Brothers program had shown him a way out, a way up. He'd made millions in the computer chip industry and then had sought a way to give back, which was how the Breckenridge Foundation had been born.

"I don't seek publicity for the work I do. I fund a select group of grassroots programs that are doing good things at the community level. When one of my staff brought StrongGirls to my attention, I knew I had to learn more about it. I was impressed at every turn, es-pecially when I found out there are only three of you. Three people, doing everything—the counseling, the administrative work. It's astounding."

"Actually, we're five now," Kat said proudly. "I had

to start small, given my funding is very modest. But the people I recruited to work with me are the best. And if the program reaches a certain level of participation by the end of the summer, the grant money increases."

"Do you mind if I ask how much?"

So she told him how her grant was structured.

He had the nerve to laugh. "You're doing the whole program on *that?*"

That? It seemed like a fortune to her. "I'm very good at stretching a dollar."

"I'll say. How would you feel about a slightly larger budget?"

Kat's heart skipped a beat. "I'd welcome an increased budget, of course. I have so many things I want to do. Like transportation. Just getting the girls to class sessions can be a challenge, when they don't even have bus fare. I'd like to be able to consult with a nutritionist. I'd like—"

"What if you had, oh, about ten times what you have now?"

Kat opened her mouth, but no words came out. Was he kidding?

Finally, she found her voice. "It sounds too good to be true. But I have to tell you that, while securing funds for the program is very important to me, I'm not ready to let it go. I'm just getting started, and I have very definite ideas of where I want the program to go. I'll take money, if it's offered. I'll account for every penny. But I'm not ready to let someone else start making the decisions."

"My dear Ms. Holiday, I'm not an idiot. StrongGirls is nothing without you. You are the program's strongest asset. I wouldn't dream of taking a single decision out of your hands. So let's get down to brass tacks. Here's what I'm offering."

Chapter Fourteen

Ethan sat out on the deck with the newspaper, keeping an eye on Samantha as she practiced her first karate form. Kat had signed her up for martial-arts classes at the rec center—something to balance out the Barbie obsession.

Samantha's focus was intense for a seven-year-old. When she got halfway through and forgot which way to kick, she stopped, and he could see her mentally reviewing the sequence of movements before starting again.

She reminded him so much of Kat, his heart ached. Would she grow up as tough on herself as Kat was? Would she learn from her mother to be strong and independent? She already showed signs of Kat's stubbornness and her compassion. Someday, would Samantha put some guy through the ringer because he loved her too much? Because he wanted to fix her life when it didn't truly need fixing?

He heard the back door open and turned to see Kat standing there, a dazed look on her face.

"Everything okay?" Ethan asked. "You look kind of funny."

Wordlessly she reached into her jacket pocket and pulled out a blue piece of paper, which she handed to Ethan.

It was a check. Ethan unfolded it. It was made out to StrongGirls, Inc., and it had a lot of zeroes on it.

"Those are gonna be some nice books."

"And that's just for starters, a stopgap measure to take some of the pressure off, while Mr. Breckenridge gets the paperwork started. He's going to give me office space and support staff. And he's going to pay for everything. Everything on my wish list and stuff I hadn't even thought to wish for. And he's giving me a salary. A huge one. I mean, ridiculous. But he said if I'm to put all my energy into growing the StrongGirl program, I don't need to be worrying about how to buy groceries or new shoes for Samantha."

Ethan looked at the check again. He'd never seen one that big before. "Can you really cash this thing?"

"I'm almost afraid to try. What if it's all a cruel joke? I feel like I've won the lottery or something." And then she burst into tears.

"Kat. Oh, honey, don't cry." He couldn't help it. He went to her and put his arms around her. God, how he'd missed this, the feel of her, the smell of her.

"It's okay," she said, her voice muffled against his chest. "They're good tears. I'm relieved, I'm grateful, I'm…overwhelmed."

"Mom, what's wrong?"

Ethan had forgotten about Samantha. She stood at the edge of the deck, watching her mother falling apart, her eyes big with fear and worry.

"Nothing's wrong," Ethan said. "For a change, everything's going right."

Well, not everything. Kat pulled away, embarrassed, wiping tears and streaked mascara from her cheeks. "I'm sorry. I got mascara on your shirt."

"Don't worry about it."

"Moooo-om," Samantha said, drawing the single syllable out to about four. "What happened?"

"You're looking at the new executive director of StrongGirls, Inc."

"Huh? What does that mean?"

"It means I don't have to wait for granola bars to go on sale!"

"This calls for a real celebration," Ethan said. "Like a party. It's not every day a bazillionaire philanthropist hands you a huge check."

"I can't have a party," Kat said, looking suddenly panic-stricken. "I have so much work to do. I have to redo all my budgets and pick out office furniture—I have to hire an assistant. I have to go shopping." She walked back into the house, muttering to herself about everything she had to do, Ethan and Samantha forgotten.

Samantha gave Ethan a puzzled look. "What's a philanthor—philander— That word you said."

"Philanthropist. It's a person with a lot of money who wants to give it away to good causes. Mr. Breckenridge is that kind of man, and he's decided Strong-Girls is a good cause."

"So he's giving us money?"

"A lot of money."

KAT WAS ALMOST ready for work one day, a week later, when Samantha came bounding into her room holding a fistful of red, white and blue ribbons. "Can you help me put these in my hair?"

"Of course. But we'll have to hurry. I have to meet the Sunset StrongGirls and I need to get you over to your grandmother's."

Samantha gave her a funny look. "You're doing StrongGirls on the Fourth of July?"

Kat's mind, which had jumped ahead to the fifth task she had planned for the day, came to a screeching halt. "July fourth? Today?" She looked at the calendar from the tire shop she'd stuck up on her wall. Sure enough, it wasn't just Monday. She sank onto her bed. "I forgot all about it."

"Mom, how could you forget? Today's the barbecue."

Oh, right. Fire Station 59 was hosting a barbecue for all the firefighters and their families. Though Kat and Samantha weren't exactly anybody's family, Priscilla, Tony and Jasmine had insisted they come.

"We're counting on you to bring your famous brownies," Tony had said the week before, when they'd talked about it.

"Samantha, you can go," Kat had agreed at the time. "But I've got so much work to do. I think I'll take advantage of the quiet house and work on my curriculum guides."

She wasn't sure, but she thought Ethan looked relieved that she'd decided not to attend the barbecue herself.

Now, Samantha wiggled so much that Kat had a hard time braiding the ribbons into her hair, but at last the task was finished.

"Mom, won't you come to the barbecue?" Samantha wheedled. "You're always working."

"I know, but—"

"Mother-daughter time," Samantha said.

Kat groaned. Her little girl sure knew which buttons to push. "I'll go for a little while, okay?" She'd pay her respects to the guys, make sure Samantha was having fun, then sneak back home.

Kat was happy to change into a pair of denim shorts and a pink T-shirt that said Born to Shop, which she'd thought funny when she bought it because it was so not her.

It felt good to shed her professional persona, and she vowed not to think about StrongGirls for at least a couple of hours and focus on being a good mom and a good friend to the people who had taken care of her and protected her during her time of need. The past week, she'd been a woman obsessed, wanting to do everything at once. She wanted to show Mr. Breckenridge that his faith in her was not misplaced, that she was going to do everything she had promised to do and more, that she was going to do great, incredible things with the money he was giving her.

She'd talked to him on the phone seven times that first day, and then promised she would stop calling him as it gradually sank in that he really was giving her the money with no strings—totally trusting her to spend it wisely. And during their last conversation, he *had* admonished her to relax and have a nice holiday.

She couldn't imagine how she'd forgotten. But now she was determined to have a good time.

Kat had brownies to bake. She'd promised. Her brownies weren't anything special, made from a box, but somehow she'd gotten this reputation for making spectacular brownies. Even Priscilla, whose high-society mother was a renowned baker, had asked her for the recipe. If they only knew.

Kat and Sam set off for the fire station on foot, but they detoured to a convenience store to buy a couple of gallons of ice cream. For the first time in a very long time, Kat didn't have to calculate the cost of everything and anguish over whether she could fit it into the budget. She just bought it.

Samantha was quivering with impatience, annoyed to miss even one minute of the party.

"You know," Kat said as they headed back out into the heat, leaving the cool shelter of the convenience store behind, "the last time we went to the fire station, you were scared to death. You wouldn't talk to any of the firefighters. Are you sure you're okay?"

"Was I really?" Samantha asked. "I don't remember."

"Right after the fire. Remember how Ethan took you out back to show you Daisy's puppies?"

Samantha thought about it. "Oh, yeah. The puppies were a lot smaller." And that was all she had to say about it. As they arrived at the door and a smiling man in a Dallas Fire and Rescue T-shirt welcomed them, Samantha showed not the slightest signs of insecurity.

"Well, look who's here," said Captain Campeon, who was officially greeting everyone as they came in. He seemed not one bit more relaxed than he had the first time Kat had seen him, his smile worn uncomfortably, as if he had to force himself to pretend to like having all these strangers wandering the fire station. He directed them through the station to the back door, where both Priscilla and Tony greeted them.

"Kat," Tony said, "we didn't think you were coming."

"Samantha twisted my arm. It's okay, isn't it?" she asked uncertainly. Maybe she wasn't welcome, after all. Maybe the invitation had been only a token one.

"Of course, you're welcome!" Tony said, showing a bit too much enthusiasm. Priscilla escorted Samantha outside to where someone was making balloon animals, but Tony all but blocked Kat's way. "Are those your brownies?"

"Yup. Still warm from the oven."

"Let's take them back to the kitchen and slice them," he said, taking her by the elbow and physically turning her around. "I don't think we have a knife outside."

Tony spent a ridiculous amount of time cutting up the brownies, claiming he wanted to get each square the same size so no one would feel slighted.

"Gee, Tony, I never noticed this perfectionist streak in you before."

"There. Done."

"Finally. Knowing you guys, if I don't get out back soon, all the barbecue will be gone."

"Not much chance of that. Jerry's parents own Wilson Meats, and they donated, like, fifty pounds of brats and chicken and ribs."

As they left the kitchen, Priscilla appeared again. She shrugged at Tony, who rolled his eyes.

What was going on with those two? Was it possible... Could they be...? Nah. If any chemistry existed between Priscilla and Tony, they'd kept it well hidden.

The fenced yard behind the fire station was seething with activity. There was a moonwalk for the kids. Daisy and her two remaining puppies were darting among the guests, a line of children chasing them. Several picnic tables had been added to the original one and covered with a red-checked oilcloth, and it was topped with enough food to feed the Dallas Cowboys for a week.

There was, indeed, a man making balloon animals. Kat recognized him as one of the firefighters she'd seen when she brought her first batch of brownies to the station.

Two teenage girls were off in a corner of the yard, hunkered down and exchanging confidences. They'd probably been dragged here against their will and thought the whole thing supremely uncool.

Kat was automatically drawn to them. In every teenage girl she saw a bit of herself—wanting to be grown-up, scared of adulthood, stretching for freedom, then shrinking back, longing for security that didn't exist in her home. She wanted to grab every teenage girl she saw and enroll her in StrongGirls. If someone had taken her in hand when she was fourteen or fifteen and given her some advice, her life would have been a lot different.

She started to drift toward the girls, but a hand on her arm stopped her.

Ethan.

"Hey, no work today. This is a holiday."

Oh, God, he looked good. His face was tanned from all the yardwork he'd been doing, his hair bleached out by the sun.

She wished he wouldn't touch her. The feel of his hand, even during an innocent moment like this, made her blood sizzle.

"I can't help it," she said. "Look at those girls. They're miserable, all alienated and angry. They need me."

"Aren't all teenage girls like that?"

"Not my StrongGirls. Maybe those girls need a job to do. Could we get them to organize some games for the younger kids?"

"Your funeral, if you want to ask them. Me, all that hormonal angst scares me to death."

"Let's just see what I can do." And she marched over to the girls, who eyed her with overt suspicion.

She plopped down on the grass next to them. "Hi, I'm Kat. What are your names?"

"Libby," came one sullen answer.

"Erin," came another.

"Y'all look kinda bored."

"Duh."

"This party is so lame, but my dad said I had to go."

"Mine, too."

"I was wondering if you girls might help me. All the younger kids are running wild, and they need a little adult supervision. Some games or something. Think you could organize a game of Mother, May I or Red Light, Green Light?"

The girls looked at each other. "I don't know how to play either of those games," said Erin.

Libby looked at her friend in stark disbelief. "You're kidding. You never played Mother, May I?"

Erin shook her head.

"It's easy," Libby said, her sudden enthusiasm chasing the sullenness from her face. "Come on, I'll show you." The girls jumped up, and Kat followed, helping them gather up the smaller kids and explaining that Erin and Libby were their new play leaders.

"I can't believe you did that," said Ethan, suddenly reappearing. He had a little girl who was about five in his arms. The big-eyed girl had a face damp from a recent bout of tears.

"It was actually easier than I thought it would be. Who's your friend?"

"This is Eva. She's Captain Campeon's niece. Eva, this is Kat."

"Hi, Eva. Do you want to play Mother, May I with the other kids? It's easy."

Eva said nothing.

"Eva has a tummy ache," Ethan said. "We're just hanging out."

Priscilla approached, looking anxious. "Kat, I'm teaching some of the guys to play bridge and we need a fourth."

"Bridge?"

"I've been threatening for weeks."

"Uh, okay."

"Yell if you need rescuing," Ethan whispered in her ear as Priscilla dragged her away.

Tony and Otis, whom Kat had gotten to know at the lake party, looked like unlikely bridge players. They sat across from each other at a card table, pondering their hands.

"Two hearts," said Otis.

"Three spades," Tony shot back.

"Oh, yeah? Five hearts."

"Six spades!"

"Seven hearts!"

"Guys, guys. Chill." Priscilla looked at Otis's hand. "You don't even have enough points to bid anything, much less a slam. Anyway, you two are partners. Let's start over."

"What's the use?" said Otis. "You're gonna beat us at this, too. Never seen anyone so lucky at cards."

Priscilla gathered up all the cards of the dog-eared deck and shuffled. "You know what they say. Lucky at cards, unlucky at love."

Otis puffed out his barrel chest. "Well, then, I oughtta be real unlucky at cards."

Kat listened to Priscilla's instructions with half an ear, her gaze wandering back to Ethan, who toted Eva around, carrying on a conversation with her. He grabbed a potato chip from a bag as he passed the picnic table, traded barbs with one of his coworkers and endured a good-natured punch on the shoulder.

Eventually, he put Eva down, and the child toddled off to join the games Libby and Erin were organizing. He joined two men presiding over the grill, engaging them in a heartfelt discussion about how to tell when a bratwurst was done.

A tightness built in Kat's chest, until it felt like a ball of raw nerves spinning where her heart was supposed to be, and then a warmth from her chest spread throughout her body, down her legs and arms and up into her face until she was sure it radiated out her ears.

"Kat?" Tony said.

"She must have some awesome cards," Otis said, "if that silly grin on her face is any indication."

Priscilla turned to see what Kat was looking at, and when she turned back, she had a knowing look on her face.

Kat was so stunned, she could barely think.

She loved Ethan. There was no doubt.

For the first time in years she and her child were safe, with no money worries. She didn't need anyone to help her with anything. She certainly didn't need Ethan to be her white knight. There was a lovely little bungalow for rent across the street from Ethan's house. Kat had already talked with the rental agent, and it was well within her budget. She could move there tomorrow, if she wanted.

And yet, her feelings for Ethan hadn't diminished at all. In fact, they were stronger than ever. How could any woman not love him? He loved kids and animals, knew how to cook, and his working life was spent saving lives and property.

She'd thought she loved Chuck. He was a good man, too, and when he offered her an escape from poverty and a future on the street, she'd jumped at the chance. He'd asked her if she loved him, and she'd said yes— even though she didn't, not quite. She'd told herself over and over that love would grow, that she couldn't expect fireworks like the ones in the movies, that that was fantasy and this was reality.

She'd been grateful to Chuck.

But the moment she'd realized she was finally secure, that she wouldn't ever again have to sleep in a homeless shelter, she also realized she didn't love Chuck and that she never would.

She loved Ethan, however, with a pure, white-hot intensity that was almost frightening. And she'd been completely stupid for breaking up with him. What had she been thinking?

"Kat, are you going to bid or not?" Priscilla asked, almost desperately. She'd been trying to distract Kat from Ethan ever since she'd arrived at the barbecue. Tony had, too, she realized, perhaps in an effort to save Ethan from any more heartache she might have in mind to dish out.

"I'm sorry, you'll have to excuse me." She was going to tell him, right now, how she felt. She was going to tell him how sorry she was for breaking things off with him. She was going to confess to being a complete idiot, and throw herself on his mercy.

She put her cards down and stood, and Tony and Otis took that as a signal that they could escape Priscilla's bridge lesson, too.

"Aw, come on, you guys, we were just getting started."

Kat extracted herself from the picnic table and headed for Ethan. He was way across the yard, which was so crowded by now that it wasn't a quick journey.

Priscilla was right behind her. "What are you doing?" she asked in a loud whisper.

"What I should have done a long time ago. I'm going to tell Ethan how I feel about him."

"Uh, I'm not so sure that's a good idea right now."

"Why not?"

But then Kat saw why not. An absolutely gorgeous Latina woman approached Ethan, and they started chatting in a friendly way.

Kat froze in her tracks, almost stumbling.

"Priscilla, who is she?"

"Tina Campeon. She's the captain's younger sister."

"Are they… She and Ethan…" What if Kat was too late?

"No, they're not," Priscilla said firmly. "They only just met today. And I can safely say Ethan has no interest in her beyond being friends. But the captain is trying to play matchmaker."

Okay, she got it. It wouldn't be cool to barge in on the captain's setup and throw herself at Ethan. But the first time she managed to get him alone…

Chapter Fifteen

TINA CAMPEON was everything the captain had promised. She was beautiful, sweet and seemed to be a devoted mom. She was an attentive date, but not clingy.

A man would have to be in his grave a year not to find her attractive. And under other circumstances, Ethan would have counted himself lucky the captain had chosen to fix *him* up with his sister.

But these weren't other circumstances. Ethan was in love with Kat, and that wasn't going to change anytime soon.

Unfortunately, Tina knew nothing about Kat—and she'd made it pretty clear that she was enjoying Ethan's company and wanted more of it. She touched him at every opportunity and smiled until his face hurt just watching her.

The captain caught up with Ethan as he went to get himself and Tina fresh cans of soda.

"So, how's it going?" he asked anxiously.

"Uh, fine, Captain. Your sister's very nice."

"Are you having a good time?"

"Sure. Her kids are really cute, too."

"I had a feeling you were a family man," the captain said, thumping Ethan on the back so hard he almost dropped the sodas. "So, do you think you'll ask her out?"

"I don't know." He couldn't lie about this, though his answer produced an immediate scowl on the captain's face. "I'm still on the rebound."

"Fine. Take your time." The captain stalked off, obviously not having gotten the answer he was looking for. Ethan knew he better watch out, or Captain Campeon would have him and Tina married off before Ethan knew what was happening. And if the romance fizzled, Ethan could look forward to years of grout and toilet scrubbing.

He returned to the table, cut up some chicken for Eva and asked Tina to tell him some stories about the beauty pageant circuit, which she seemed happy to do.

"Do you know, I had to put duct tape on my heinie?" Then she added in a whisper, "So it wouldn't wiggle. Oops, I probably shouldn't tell you stuff like that."

Ethan laughed. She was really a funny, delightful woman. Maybe Tony would ask her out. She certainly deserved better than Ethan, who would never be able to focus all of his attention on her while his heart was somewhere else. Yeah, Tony was dating Daralee, the woman from the church fire, but the end of that relationship was already in sight.

"So what's it like working for my brother?" Tina asked.

Pure hell. Fortunately, Ethan was saved from answering when the alarm went off.

He put down his knife and fork. "That's my cue."

"Oh, Ethan, be careful."

"I'm always careful." And with that he was gone, to the apparatus room to don his turnout gear.

His adrenaline surged as word came over the radio—there was a real fire, a house fire, fully involved.

So far, Kat's apartment building was the only serious fire Ethan had fought. He realized it would be years before he would go on a call like this and not be terrified.

It took them only three minutes to reach the fire, and it was a beaut. A large frame house had smoke pouring out almost every one of its boarded-up windows. He hoped to hell the place wasn't occupied.

Engine 59 was the first to arrive, and Captain Campeon was right behind him driving the ladder truck. Campeon assumed command of the situation. "The structure isn't even stable at this point," he barked out. "Neighbors report the house was unoccupied, and the house itself probably isn't salvageable. Our highest priority is to keep nearby structures from igniting."

He might not be the most pleasant man in the world, but he thought fast on his feet.

Other engines arrived, but Ethan focused on his task. He and Murph McCrae, who'd finally reconciled himself to having a rookie at his elbow, were to locate the utility shutoff valves and disconnect them all.

These big, old houses sometimes had more than one cutoff, if the place had been broken up into apartments. Fortunately, Murph went right to the gas.

"You work enough fires, you get an instinct about

where to look." He stood back and let Ethan do the actual work.

Ethan had just turned the valve when he heard something—coughing, a strangled cry—coming from inside.

They'd been told the house was empty. Had he imagined the sound?

He looked at the lieutenant. Murph had heard it, too, and he was already grabbing for his radio.

"Engine Fifty-nine to Incident Command. There's someone inside, I can hear him. Request permission to execute a primary search."

"Engine Fifty-nine, affirmative," came the reply.

Murph had an ax, and he used it attack the rotting plywood covering one of the windows, quickly reducing it to splinters. Smoke wafted out.

Ethan hoisted himself up onto the bottom of the window frame and tried to see in.

"I can see the guy," Ethan said. But the smoke was getting thicker, and soon all he could make out was a pair of bare feet attached to someone who was clearly incapacitated.

Murph cursed. "Wait for me, eager beaver. I'm bigger than you."

Ethan waited, but he called to the victim, trying to get a response.

There, he heard it again, the feeble groan. The guy was alive. Ethan dropped to his hands and knees, and Murph was soon beside him. Down low, it was clear enough to see with his flashlight. He spotted the bare feet again.

"Over here," he said. He and Murph crawled to the victim, who appeared to be an old man who'd been squatting in the vacant house, if a pile of nasty bedding and garbage sack of aluminum cans nearby were any indication.

He was still conscious, and Ethan grasped him by the shoulders and started dragging. When the old guy yelled in protest, Ethan realized the floor was covered with burning embers. They dropped from above like hail from hell.

Ethan hoisted the man over his shoulder. It seemed the fastest way.

"Let's get out of here," Murph yelled. "I don't like the looks of that—" Before he could even finish the sentence, something cracked overhead. Ethan went as fast as he could toward the window, then realized he couldn't see it. He'd become disoriented, and standing up where the smoke was thicker, he couldn't see a damn thing.

Murph grabbed his arm. "This way."

Thank God. The ceiling was about to come down. Embers had turned to burning chunks of wood and plaster.

They reached the bright light of the window, which appeared out of nowhere. Murph climbed through first, and then Ethan shoved out the old man, who was making enough noise to let them know he was still breathing and not very happy about leaving behind his stash of aluminum cans. Murph cursed, as the old man kicked at him and they both fell to the ground outside. Not the prettiest rescue, but mission accomplished.

Ethan had just braced his hands against the window

frame to climb out himself, when an unholy noise from above made him look up. Too late he realized he should have just dived through the hole. A four-by-four beam was heading straight for him.

That was the last conscious thought he had.

THE MOOD OF THE Fire Station 59 picnic had grown somber. The smaller kids, not realizing what was going on, still ran and shrieked, but the adults had gone quiet.

Every firefighter and paramedic on the C shift had cleared out to help fight the fire, and even some of the off-duty guys had taken off, leaving their families to wait.

By now, everybody knew it was a pretty big fire. They could see the smoke in the distance. And all Kat could think about was that Ethan was there.

What if he was hurt? What if something happened to him, and she never had the chance to tell him she loved him?

Tina Campeon sidled up to her. "I don't think we've met. I'm Tina."

"Kat Holiday." Kat did her best to smile. It wasn't Tina's fault that she was gaga over Ethan. She probably had no way of knowing Kat had a history with her new boyfriend.

"I'm Eric Campeon's sister," Tina said. "What's your connection?"

"I'm a firefighter's roommate," Kat said.

"You're not married to one of them, then?"

"No."

"I don't know how the wives do it. I mean, I guess

if you're at home, you don't know when the alarms go off. You don't see them run for the trucks and ride off to risk their lives. This is kind of freaky."

"I agree, it is." If she and Ethan got back together, she would worry about him every time he walked out of the house to work. But even if they didn't work things out…she still would worry. She hoped she got the chance to learn to live with it.

"At least we don't have as many serious fires as in the past. Eric said they use safer building materials now." Tina drummed her fingernails on the table. "But it doesn't make this waiting any easier."

Kat found herself liking the woman. At least they had something in common—they both had a thing for Ethan.

No one went home. Some of the smaller kids flopped down on quilts and napped in the heat, but everyone else hung around.

An hour passed, and then two, which was way too long. Some of the off-duty firefighters had gone in to listen to the radio, and whispers soon filtered back to Kat.

Someone was injured. A firefighter was down. No one seemed to know who it was, however.

A profound sense of misery descended on Kat, and somehow she knew—she just knew—that it was Ethan. And she vowed to heaven that if he came through this, when she saw him the first words out of her mouth were going to be, "I love you."

When the engine returned, its crew grimy, stinky and exhausted from fighting the fire, Kat stayed well away from it. She didn't want to know. But after a few minutes, Priscilla came and sat next to her, ominously silent. Her face was smudged black and she smelled of smoke.

"Pris," Kat said, "tell me."

"Ethan was hurt," Priscilla finally said, the words coming out as if they'd been dragged. "We don't know how bad. Something fell on him. They took him to the hospital. Tony's with him. That's all I know about his condition."

Kat closed her eyes and let the fear wash over her, rather than fighting it. Ethan was injured. But he wasn't dead—the news could have been worse. "Was it arson?" she asked. From hanging out with firefighters, Kat knew that the serial arsonist was never far from their minds. Everyone was wondering if or when he'd hit again.

"They think it was a squatter's cook stove."

"Was anyone else injured?" Kat asked.

"Just the squatter, an old man. No one knew he was there. Ethan heard him. He and Murph went inside after him and Ethan carried him out. He was almost out himself when the ceiling above him came down. He probably shouldn't have gone in."

"I doubt anything in the world would have stopped him," Kat said. "Not his training, not fear. He can't stand to see anyone in pain."

"I know." She paused, reflecting on something. "The engine hit a squirrel once. After we got done with the call, Ethan wanted to go back and see if the squirrel was okay."

"Was it?"

"No, it was dead. Ethan hardly talked to anyone the rest of the day."

Kat couldn't help smiling through the tears. Ethan did notice the dead squirrels. He always felt a little bad for them.

"Pris, I've made a terrible mistake," Kat said. "I should never have let Ethan go."

"It's not too late to change your mind."

"But what if it is?"

Priscilla grew solemn at the grim reminder. "Maybe you should go to the hospital."

ETHAN FELT AS IF someone had put an ax through his head and maybe landed a few blows on his neck and shoulders, too. He had no idea where he was or what had happened to him, but he didn't dare move or open his eyes.

It seemed much safer to lie very still. Maybe he would drift back into the place he'd been before, the place where he didn't hurt, where every breath wasn't an effort.

But he couldn't reclaim oblivion. In fact, the harder he tried, the more he became aware of various sensations—an annoying, insistent beeping coming from somewhere behind him. The smell of disinfectant. The hard surface beneath him.

And the fact he couldn't move.

He reached the inevitable conclusion he was in a hospital. That or hell. But he preferred the more optimistic choice. He still had no idea how he'd gotten here. But he recognized a painkiller haze when he felt one. He'd been given morphine once before, when he'd had his appendix out as a teenager.

He also recognized that the haze was lifting. His thinking was becoming more clear. And the pain was getting worse. He wondered if he would have to ask to get more drugs or if they were giving them through a drip. He focused on his arm. He tried to move it.

To his surprise, the muscles responded. But the arm was restrained. And yes, he could feel the needle.

"Ethan?"

An angel. What was an angel doing here? This could be very bad news.

"Are you awake? I saw you move."

It wasn't an angel. It was Kat. Nothing could have motivated him more to return to the land of the living.

"Mmph."

"Oh, Ethan, you *are* awake."

"Sort of."

"Thank God. Okay, just listen for a minute, because I swore that the moment you were conscious, I had to tell you something, so here it is. I love you. I guess I've loved you all along, but I got confused about whether I *really* loved you or just needed you."

This wasn't hell. This was heaven, pain and all. Unless he was hallucinating.

"Wha——" His voice cracked, his throat dry as a drought-ravaged field. He tried again. "What happened?"

"You don't remember?"

Would he be asking, if he remembered?

"You went to a fire. You rescued a homeless man."

He did? No matter how hard he tried, he couldn't recall anything about a homeless man.

"The Fourth of July picnic?"

No. He remembered getting ready for the picnic. A checkered tablecloth, a pile of uncooked meat, waiting for the grill.

"How about Tina Campeon? Remember her?"

Tina. The captain's sister. "I don't remember her."

"Good. Let's keep it that way."

Ethan was finally brave enough to crack his eyes open. It wasn't as bad as he'd feared. The light was low in his room or cubicle or wherever this was. And there was Kat, her face inches from his, looking more beautiful than he'd ever seen her look.

He tried for a smile. "Kat." Had she said she loved him? Surely that was his memory playing tricks on him. He'd been clunked on the head. He couldn't trust his mind to work properly.

"I was supposed to have a date with Tina."

Kat sighed. "You did have a date. And I can't lie— Tina is gorgeous, she's very nice, she has two darling children, and you two were getting along like—"

"Like a house on fire?"

"I wasn't going to say that."

"I only talked to her to make the captain happy." He winced as a spear of pain shot through him.

"Oh, Ethan, you're hurting. I'll get a nurse."

"No. No, I don't want any more drugs right now. I want to understand what happened."

"The alarm sounded during the picnic," Kat said patiently. She looked so cute in her little pink T-shirt. Born to Shop. Yeah, right. "You went to a burning house. A man was trapped inside—"

"Yeah, I got that part. Why are you here?"

"Because I care about you."

"That's not how you said it earlier."

"Because I love you."

Ethan closed his eyes and settled back against his pillow. He hadn't imagined it. Everything would be okay now. He drifted off again.

The next time he awoke, the experience was far less pleasant. There was a doctor shouting questions at him, as if he were hard of hearing, and a nurse messing with his IV and changing a bandage on his head. He did learn a little more about his injuries—a severe concussion and a compressed vertebra, which explained why he was immobilized. His turnout gear—and Murph's quick actions—had saved him from any serious burns. The doctor expected him to make a full recovery.

He still had no memory of the fire, the old man he'd dragged out of the house or even the barbecue, other than the early preparations. The doctor said he might never regain any of those memories, but that that was normal with a severe concussion.

He wondered how his date with Tina had gone. He wasn't sure he could trust Kat's impressions. She loved him, after all. He grinned as he recalled her obvious jealousy.

"You look pretty happy for a man in your shape," said his nurse, who'd been entertaining him with wise-cracks since she came on duty.

"I'm in love," Ethan said. "I feel no pain."

"Sorry to disappoint you, but I'm taken."

"Well, shoot."

Another female voice chimed in. "If you're talkin' about Kat, she's been haunting this place like a ghost. I can fetch her, now that you're awake."

"Mom? What are you doing here?"

"Tony called me."

That figured. "He shouldn't have bothered you. I don't like for you to worry."

"Don't you be tellin' me if I can worry or not," she scolded. "And I'd worry a lot more if I thought no one would call me when you're hurt." Her voice softened. "Are you okay? Need anything?" She leaned into his line of vision, and he wished she hadn't. She looked like she'd just come off a hard night of drinking, except he knew she was a teetotaler.

"Mom, I'm okay."

"I know, Ethan." She smoothed the hair off his forehead. "You're always there for everyone else. Now, I hope you'll let others take care of you."

"Doesn't look like I have much choice." He had feeling in his arms and legs, much to his relief, but he was literally tied down to the bed. "Mom, I need to see Kat, if she's still around." He hadn't been at his most eloquent the first time she'd visited, but he'd do better this time.

His mom left, and a few minutes later someone else

entered his cubicle. He couldn't turn his head to see who it was, so he inhaled. Ah, yes. Kat.

"I love you, too, you know," he said without preamble.

"Oh. Oh. Ethan, at least give me some warning." She grasped his hand, her fingers warm and reassuring, and he did his best to squeeze back. Then she sobbed, and he didn't know what to do.

"Kat, don't cry. You know I can't stand it when you cry. Aren't we supposed to be happy?"

"It's just that I came so close to losing you."

"I wasn't going to go off with Tina."

"How do you know? You don't remember her. Maybe you instantly fell in love with her, and the two of you were planning your elopement."

"She's not here, is she?" He didn't want to face Tina, no matter how beautiful or sweet the woman was. He didn't want to have to tell her that it wasn't going to work out between them because he was madly in love with someone else.

"Anyway, I mean I almost lost you, literally. The fire."

"I wasn't hurt that bad."

"Yeah, sure. You have to promise me you'll stop being such a hero. You know what they're calling you? Mr. Rescue."

He laughed and it hurt, so he stopped. He wondered if he had broken ribs on top of his other injuries. The doctor hadn't mentioned it, but maybe broken ribs were considered inconsequential, given everything else.

"You've had two big fires in your whole career, and both times you saved people's lives. You're making the other guys look bad."

Ethan doubted that. He'd probably done something stupid. He was probably going to get yelled at for weeks on end—if not for getting injured, then for being a lousy date for the captain's baby sister.

He didn't care. Kat loved him.

"Kat, if getting injured made you realize you love me, I'll get hurt every day of my life."

"Bite your tongue. And that's not what did it."

"Then what changed your mind?"

"My mind never changed. I always loved you. I think it started the day you told me you'd given Bashira a bath. But I didn't trust myself. I'd deluded myself once before, and it was so unfair to Chuck. I couldn't bear the thought of repeating that mistake. You'd rescued me—literally saved my life and my daughter's life. Of course I would have very strong feelings toward you. But how was I to know if it was real love or something else masquerading as love because I needed you?"

"So when did you figure it out?"

"At the barbecue. I realized that for the first time in years, I was safe and secure, and I didn't need anyone to take care of me or feed me or shelter me. Yet I still felt exactly the same way toward you. I saw you with that little girl, Tina's daughter…"

"I was with Tina's daughter?"

"She had a tummy ache. You were carrying her around, trying to make her feel better, and it hit me like a ton of bricks. And I went straight for you. I was playing bridge with Pris and Tony and Otis—"

"Otis was playing *bridge?*"

"I dropped everything and made a beeline for you," she continued, ignoring the interruption, "because I was going to tell you I loved you. And then there was Tina, and the alarm went off… And I swore that the next time I saw you, I'd tell you straight away."

She was adorable. "If I could get out of this bed and put my arms around you right now, I would, and I'd never let you go. Ever."

"Even if I'm a flake who doesn't know her own mind?"

"You're not a flake, and I love you. There's just one problem."

"What?"

"No, never mind, I'll take care of it. I'll move out."

"What?" she said again, only more emphatically. "Why?"

"Because you have this thing about living with your boyfriend. Bad example for the StrongGirls."

"I have a thing about *moving in* with my boyfriend, when I have nowhere else to go. I have a thing about letting my boyfriend rescue me. Still, you have a point. I don't feel there's anything wrong with two committed adults co-habiting, but the situation could be misconstrued."

"So I'll move out."

"No! That's ridiculous—it's your house. Samantha and I can rent that cute bungalow across the street."

He thought about that for a moment, thought about

his house without Kat, without the whisper of her scent in every room, the sound of her humming while she cooked, without Samantha's laughter. It wasn't a pleasant picture.

But how could he stop her? The answer came to him immediately, and it made perfect sense. "I have a better idea. Why don't we just get married?"

Silence. Ominous silence. Hell, he'd blown it. Wasn't that just like him? He finally gets Kat to admit she loves him, but that wasn't good enough. He had to push.

"Kat, forget I said anything."

"Forget it?" Her voice came out a squeak. "You're taking it back?"

"You didn't respond."

"Because I was so overcome. Because Samantha will be delirious. Damn, I'm not a StrongGirl, after all. Look at me—I'm a mess."

"I can't look at you. I can't turn my head."

"Good. My nose is probably all red, and my eyes are puffing up."

"Is that a yes?"

"Yes."

Epilogue

A fire station was hardly the most romantic venue for a wedding. But there was no way to pick a date when at least some of Ethan's newfound friends weren't going to be on duty, and they all wanted to witness history in the making—one of their own marrying a woman he'd dragged out of a burning building.

So Kat, with the help of Priscilla, Deb and Virginia, and plenty of legwork by StrongGirls from three high schools, had turned the backyard of Fire Station 59 into an oasis of flowers, with an arbor and ribbons—and citronella torches to keep the mosquitoes at bay.

Kat was upstairs in the station's dormitory area getting dressed, and every so often she peeked out a window as the yard filled up. Every chair was taken, and people were standing in the back.

"Where did all these people come from?" Kat asked Priscilla, who was doing up the buttons on the back of Kat's candlelight chiffon dress. "I only sent out a few invitations."

"I'm afraid your wedding has turned into a bona fide media event," Priscilla replied.

"Really. Hey, I bet I can use this to publicize the StrongGirls program."

"Get your mind off your work, girl," Virginia scolded as she fussed with Kat's veil. "You're about to marry Prince Charming."

Kat sighed. "You're right. I can't help it, though. I love the StrongGirls. You know, the Sunset girls pitched in and gave me a wedding gift. A toaster. Isn't that sweet?"

"Mom," said Samantha, who'd been dressed for hours in her ruffled princess dress, claiming she felt just like Barbie. She was looking out a different window, where valets were parking the guests' cars. The valets had been a gift from the three shift captains, who could not risk a traffic jam around the station. "A big black car just pulled up. It has, like, eight windows."

Kat clapped her hands together. "Mr. Breckenridge. I was hoping he would come."

"I wonder what sort of wedding gift you'll get from him?" Priscilla asked. "Stop wiggling and let me finish your dress."

Kat stood as still as she could. "I told him I wanted an omelet pan."

The ceremony was short and sweet by design. Though it was only ten in the morning, it was already hot as blazes—this was July in Texas, after all. A big striped canopy protected the wedding party and guests from the worst of the direct sun, but it still wasn't exactly comfortable.

Kat had no trouble with a quick wedding. She felt no jitters at all, other than a perfectly normal case of nerves about everyone staring at her. She now knew her mind, and she knew it well.

Ethan looked spectacular in his tux. He was still on medical leave and would be for a few more weeks, but he hadn't wanted to postpone the wedding and neither had Kat. She'd wasted enough time with her waffling.

They said their vows, Ethan took Kat's ring from Tony, his best man, and in a matter of a few short minutes, Ethan and Kat were husband and wife. They kissed and everyone applauded, with no small number of catcalls from the ever-sensitive firefighters.

A cake in the shape of a fire engine was wheeled out, and Kat groaned. She'd put Priscilla in charge of the cake, trusting that the matter would be taken care of with taste and refinement. She shot Priscilla an accusing look, but Priscilla just beamed innocently, as if she'd had nothing to do with the unconventional cake.

"It better taste good," Kat called over her shoulder as Ethan tugged her toward the cake. Written in icing was the lovely sentiment, "Best wishes, Kat and Mr. Rescue."

When Kat and Ethan cut into it, she discovered it was a red velvet cake, which seemed appropriate. And it *was* delicious. They drank nonalcoholic champagne, since no alcohol was allowed at the fire station.

A hush fell over the crowd when Tony stood on a chair to make a toast. "To my best friend, Ethan," he said, with uncharacteristic solemnity. "He saved my life when I was ten, and he's been saving people ever since.

"I'm sure most of you know how Ethan and Kat met, so I won't repeat the story. But what many of you might not know is that Kat saves people, too. She works with young women, many that society would have forgotten if not for Kat. Ethan pulls people out of burning buildings. Kat pulls them out of a different kind of trouble."

Kat was touched. She hadn't realized Tony paid that much attention to what she did for a living, or thought about the similarities in their jobs.

"God only knows what these two can do as a team," Tony continued. "All I can say is, everybody stand back."

Everyone broke into applause, and the StrongGirls cheered louder than anyone. Kat had sworn she wasn't going to cry on this happy day, but she did anyway.

A siren sounded, and everyone jumped out of habit. But it wasn't the normal alarm. Kat and Ethan looked around for the source of the noise.

Ripples of laughter and surprise moved through the guests. "Ah. Look." Ethan pointed to the street. Just beyond the fence was an antique fire engine, festooned with bows and balloons and, yes, tin cans and old firemen's boots tied to the back.

Captain Campeon strode up to them, looking uncharacteristically pleased with himself. "The guys— and Priscilla—chipped in and rented it. You've got an hour, for the wedding party to joyride."

It was an unconventional ending, befitting their bizarre wedding. Ethan, Kat, Tony, Priscilla and Samantha climbed on board the 1940s-era fire engine—

which came equipped with a driver, thank heavens—and went for a spin around Oak Cliff. Children ran out to wave and cheer, and adults stopped what they were doing to smile at the bride and groom.

Kat felt a huge wave of love—for Ethan, for her friends, for her daughter, for the firefighters who'd come through for them, and for the checkerboard community that was Oak Cliff. Despite the patches of poverty and urban decay here and there, she saw the good that was manifested through the efforts of people like Ethan, Tony and Priscilla, and by her own work.

She would accomplish good things here. But not alone. She would give help when it was needed, and accept help when offered. She was a StrongGirl, but she was also part of a team, which meant she'd never have to stand alone again.

* * * * *

Watch for Tony's story, HER PERFECT HERO,
the next book in the
FIREHOUSE 59 series, coming February 2007
only from Harlequin American Romance.

Happily ever after is just the beginning...

Turn the page for a sneak preview of
DANCING ON SUNDAY AFTERNOONS
by
Linda Cardillo

Harlequin Everlasting—Every great love
has a story to tell.™
A brand-new line from Harlequin Books
launching this February!

Prologue

Giulia D'Orazio
1983

I had two husbands—Paolo and Salvatore.

Salvatore and I were married for thirty-two years. I still live in the house he bought for us; I still sleep in our bed. All around me are the signs of our life together. My bedroom window looks out over the garden he planted. In the middle of the city, he coaxed tomatoes, peppers, zucchini—even grapes for his wine—out of the ground. On weekends, he used to drive up to his cousin's farm in Waterbury and bring back manure. In the winter, he wrapped the peach tree and the fig tree with rags and black rubber hoses against the cold, his massive, coarse hands gentling those trees as if they were his fragile-skinned babies. My neighbor, Dominic Grazza, does that for me now. My boys have no time for the garden.

In the front of the house, Salvatore planted roses. The roses I take care of myself. They are giant, cream-colored, fragrant. In the afternoons, I like to sit out on the porch with my coffee, protected from the eyes of the neighborhood by that curtain of flowers.

Salvatore died in this house thirty-five years ago. In the last months, he lay on the sofa in the parlor so he could be in the middle of everything. Except for the two oldest boys, all the children were still at home and we ate together every evening. Salvatore could see the dining room table from the sofa, and he could hear everything that was said. "I'm not dead, yet," he told me. "I want to know what's going on."

When my first grandchild, Cara, was born, we brought her to him, and he held her on his chest, stroking her tiny head. Sometimes they fell asleep together.

Over on the radiator cover in the corner of the parlor is the portrait Salvatore and I had taken on our twenty-fifth anniversary. This brooch I'm wearing today, with the diamonds—I'm wearing it in the photograph also—Salvatore gave it to me that day. Upstairs on my dresser is a jewelry box filled with necklaces and bracelets and earrings. All from Salvatore.

I am surrounded by the things Salvatore gave me, or did for me. But, God forgive me, as I lie alone now in my bed, it is Paolo I remember.

Paolo left me nothing. Nothing, that is, that my family, especially my sisters, thought had any value. No house. No diamonds. Not even a photograph.

But after he was gone, and I could catch my breath from the pain, I knew that I still had something. In the middle of the night, I sat alone and held them in my hands, reading the words over and over until I heard his voice in my head. I had Paolo's letters.

* * * * *

Be sure to look for
DANCING ON SUNDAY AFTERNOONS
available January 30, 2007.
And look, too, for our other Everlasting title
available, FALL FROM GRACE by Kristi Gold.

FALL FROM GRACE is a deeply emotional story
of what a long-term love really means.
As Jack and Anne Morgan discover, marriage
vows can be broken—but they can be mended,
too. And the memories of their marriage have
an unexpected power to bring back a love
that never really left....